BRIGHTER LATER

By
Joaquina Ballard Howles

Also by Joaquina Ballard Howles

No More Giants

Copyright © 2020 Joaquina Ballard Howles.

The moral right of the author has been asserted.

All rights reserved.

No part of this book can be reproduced in any form or by written, electronic or mechanical, including photocopying, recording, or by any information retrieval system without written permission in writing by the author.

This is a work of fiction. Names, characters and events described herein are the work of the author's imagination. Any resemblance to actual persons, living or dead, or to real events, is entirely coincidental.

Although every precaution has been taken in the preparation of this book, the author assumes no responsibility for errors or omissions. Neither is any liability assumed for damages resulting from the use of information contained herein.

Gale force winds, driving rain, sleet at times, brighter later.

BBC Weather Forecast

In memory of Anthony Close

"Tony"

Brave beloved son-in-law

With special thanks to:

Jeffrey Brock, Park Superintendant
Richmond Park

Barry Fazackerley, Senior Prosthetic Manager
Queen Mary's University Hospital, Roehampton

Dr Brian Horne, Lecturer in Theology
King's College, London

The Revd James Naters, Father Superior
Society of St John the Evangelist

Dr Ivan Walton, Senior Consultant
Charing Cross Hospital

I

Fear. The driving force in the universe. Or is it love? The opposites are not love and hate, but love and fear. That simple. That basic. And that powerful.

In the end it was the fear of murder that sent Marinda for help. She was afraid to go to the police knowing it would have been useless; she had read enough to know they were always powerless until afterwards, until they had a body or blood or actual witnesses to threats, and as yet there were none of these. It would be too late when there was anything more concrete.

Walking fast - no need to run now that she was out of the house - she was more in control with every step as she reached the car, unlocked it quickly and slipped into the driver's seat, releasing the great ragged gasp of relief she had not known she was holding back until then. The central lock clicked to the touch of her fingers and she was enveloped in a cocoon of safety, immediate and complete. She bowed her head for a moment on the steering wheel, waiting for the muffled pounding in her chest to lessen, her breathing to regularize. It did not matter that she was uncertain of her destination, she would simply drive as she worked it out, temporarily safe in this womb of warmth, lulled by the comforting smell of metal and leather. For a time at least the fear would recede. For a time at least she would not have to think.

She pulled away from the kerb slowly, secure now in the mere fact of motion, and glanced at the petrol gauge. Enough. Three quarters of a tank was more than enough for wherever she decided to go. She started down Glebe

Road first with its wide trees and wide houses, turning left past the pub with its hanging baskets of flowers, then left again past the pond and into the road that ran beside the Common.

Now she had entered a tunnel of trees, a waterfall of trees, golden with sunlight dripping through the leaves to lie on the road in pools of gold. Breathtakingly beautiful. The inner panic was receding; she was becoming part of the world again. A parked row of commuter cars lined the edge of the miniature woodland where the road forked to a branch railway station. She even smiled at the glimpse of pseudo-Elizabethan chimneys rising above the trees, more like a garden folly or a Hansel-and-Gretel cottage in a fairy tale than a British Rail station. The trains came thick and fast during the morning and evening rush hours but now in the mid afternoon there was nothing, no sound, no one in sight except a woman in the distance walking a dog. The scene was so quietly rural it was hard to believe it was still in London. If she had painted it exactly as it was, calling it, "Country Scene", no one would have been any the wiser.

She would have had to buy another tube of titanium white, however, and several shades of yellow to capture the gold that was everywhere this afternoon en masse, mixed with sunlight. She had seldom seen so much gold at once, it was in the air, it was beside her, it was beneath her in that briefest of autumn periods when as many leaves lie on the ground as wait on the branches above. They would not last long. Two or three days at most, less if a high wind came.

But just for now the sunlight caught and drenched, magnified, reflected, glowed and glittered on all of them, singly and together, above and below. It also glittered on occasional piles of broken glass beside the commuter cars where the windows had been smashed and the radios ripped out and stolen. Even here, even in Barnes, safest and most middle class of London's villages, was this reminder of the eternal dichotomy, the contradiction of a beautiful, bent and broken world.

She sighed, feeling again the jagged edge of her own fear, edging the car onward with hands clenched tight and white on the steering wheel. Even this sunlight was temporary, more so than the leaves. The sun would sink, but long before it did the cast of light itself would change, was changing even now, this beauty-engendered euphoria would vanish, transmute into the unbearably sad light of late afternoon. What then? Was there safety anywhere? Where after all could she go?

She tried not to think ahead, into a future which did not exist. She could only deal with the present, and for now this place was as good as any. Her fear had been tranquillized by an injection of beauty, however temporary, and she wanted more, wanted to extend the respite. The way an alcoholic does, she thought bitterly.

She was calmer now, yes, but she could not procrastinate forever, sooner or later she would have to make a plan. Escape would not be easy nor perhaps even possible. The clock on the dashboard read 2:27. She drove slowly out of the trees, away from the frenzied beauty of the Common.

If she stayed on Vine Road, Richmond Park would be only a traffic light away and that would be a good idea surely; she loved the country feel of its hills and open spaces, the herds of deer, the ancient oak trees. Legend had it that Henry VIII was hunting in Richmond Park (a century before its wall and name) when he heard the single cannon fired from the Tower of London to signal the beheading of Anne Boleyn. It was as well to remember there had been women worse off than she was herself, women who had met death before at the whim of a cold and ruthless man. She was glad not to be Anne Boleyn, waiting, watching her own scaffold being built outside the window. She shook her head back into the present as she entered the park gates. She did not want to think of Anne Boleyn. That was dangerous ground. If she was avoiding the future, she should also avoid the past.

Instead she pushed a tape into the radio, flicked the switch to the comforting repetitive sound of baroque music, and slowed to pass the red deer grazing near the road. It was a herd of perhaps eighteen, a king and his harem. In the distance to her left she could see another herd among the bracken, but these were the small dappled fallow deer. She used to think they were fawns, baby-spotted like Bambi, but had learned this was not so; they were a separate breed who strangely enough, did not mate with the others, these "Monarchs of the Glen" she was passing now.

It was these Henry VIII would have been hunting, these big red deer, hunting with his bow and arrows, his courtiers and his magnificent horses swooping after them in full pursuit. Heavy running hooves would have sounded on the soil, reverberating against the lighter, quicker, frightened hoofbeats of the deer - like timpani in a terrible parody of symphony, she thought, but in a time before symphony had been invented. So that thought, like her own life perhaps, was out of kilter. She closed her eyes momentarily.

Hoofbeats, yes, and there would have been shouting from the gaily clad courtiers, hoarse masculine shouts as they reined in their horses to the stringed pluck of the King's bow (violins?) and the swishing sound of the arrow. For there would have been only the one arrow, the King's, the first choice as the others held back, the arrow singing and winging its way to the deer amid the cheers of the men. And then over it all would have sounded the distant thud of the cannon. And Henry VIII would have known that the once-loved dark head of the wife still in her twenties was finally severed, had fallen bloodily into the basket placed to catch it in front of the chopping block.

Did he really hear the cannon, nearly ten miles away in the Tower of London? Perhaps he did. There were no distracting planes in the sky as now, no constant background drone of traffic. And if he did, did he smile when he heard it, grimly satisfied?

And she? Did she, in that split second of awareness after the sword had struck, with her vision upside down in her falling head - was it fear she felt or love? A massive fear for what had already happened, the worst - or since it had already happened did it free her for a micro-second of love? Love for the life she was losing, for the world she was leaving, for God himself perhaps - or for Henry, whom she had once also loved as a god as well as a man? Impossible, for to love she would have had to forgive, and how could that be? For there had been a child as well, only three years old - seven years younger than Heather - and it had made no difference. Ah, but it had been a female child and that had made a difference.

Poor Anne Boleyn, trapped forever in a tangle of love and fear, trapped in her time and in time itself. Four hundred years ago it was not only unthinkable but impossible to defy the King, there was no press, there was no appeal. Four hundred years ago there would have been no car in which to escape as she was escaping, in which to drive through Richmond Park as she herself was driving now. But supposing there had been? Suppose miraculously Anne had found herself in this very car - oh, how gladly Marinda would have lent it to her - what would Anne have done if she had come across Henry at this very moment right here on this knoll, already dismounted from his horse, standing frowning beside his kill, and she in her car?

Savagely Marinda accelerated, pointing the car beyond the herd of deer towards the slope which led to Richmond Gate. It was a long gradual incline and she half perceived a single deer further on to her right, large and perilously near the road, but she did not slow down.

Her thoughts were of Henry VIII but it was Michael's face which appeared before her suddenly unbidden, disembodied, real as a hologram, Michael's face with its cruel, taunting smile, superimposed across the deer. The sun flashed straight into her eyes as she felt the soft thump of the body thrown over the bonnet, one antler caught in the left wing-mirror as the deer slumped down in the bellow of a great moan.

"Oh God, dear God!" She locked the brake and leapt from the car, struggling to release the antler from the side mirror where the animal hung, its neck at a grotesque angle. Clutching one branch of the horn she could feel its entire weight - so heavy, how heavy! - and was dimly aware of the superhuman strength surging through her own hands, knowing in that instant she could lift the entire animal if she had to. But it was the mirror which gave way instead, breaking off as the deer slid to the ground, still bellowing, its eyes wide with terror.

Frantically she looked about for help, for anything, another person, another car - usually there was so much traffic in the park - but there was nothing. How could there be nothing? No, wait - an old red mini was approaching now from the opposite direction. She waved both arms but he was already stopping, stepping out of the car, a young man with red bushy hair in a T-shirt and jeans, old enough and young enough to be her son Octavian, his mouth open in astonishment.

"Do you have a phone?" She knew it was a silly question as she asked it; the car was an old one, mobile phones the newest of the new luxuries and the boy most likely unemployed anyway to be driving through the park at this hour in the afternoon. And why on earth was she thinking such silly pointless thoughts with part of her mind when the other part should be - and was - concerned with what had happened?

"I've hit a deer," she said, properly distraught.

The young man who had been shaking his head, now nodded, glancing nervously from her to the deer which had stopped moaning and was scratching the ground in a feeble attempt to rise. "Is he dying?"

"I don't know. I think so. I've got to get help. I've got to report it to somebody. Only I don't know -" she looked around distractedly as if she might see a passing RSPCA van or a fire engine.

"There's the gatehouse." The boy pointed back the way she had come. "Maybe somebody there could help."

7

"Yes." It made sense. "Yes, of course." She opened the car door, then hesitated, looking at the deer which was still desperately but silently trying to rise. She was glad there was no blood and hoped that meant it might live. Its head was on the ground where little puffs of dust arose with each snort from its nostrils.

"I'll stay with him," the young man pointed with the toe of his trainers, "until you get back."

"Oh, please," she nodded, looking at the anxious blue eyes and slightly protruding buck teeth. "I mean, thank you." He was older than she had thought, perhaps twenty-eight, and he was all right, obviously an animal lover himself.

For the first time it occurred to her to look at her own car, the crumpled wing and shattered headlight. But it was driveable. Other cars were approaching now.

"They'll think it's a hit-and-run," she muttered as she jolted the car into reverse, turning to retrace the hill. By now she had begun to shake so much that driving itself was difficult, but it was not far to the little gatehouse with its curtains and dark green door and the inscription VR1 - 1900 set high up in its red brick wall. She had never paid the building any attention before, but now hoped frantically that someone would be at home.

No one was. Or if they were, she would not have dared disturb them, for the tall sign planted just inside the looped iron fence warned that the lodge was a private residence and that all enquiries were to be directed to the Royal Parks Police via the adjacent emergency phone.

And there across the road, half hidden by foliage, was

a square pillar of yellow brick with a wooden door and another sign advising that the telephone inside was for emergency use only, but that "Officers and cars respond to urgent calls." She opened the door and seized the receiver. Surely this qualified as an urgent call?

"Royal Parks Constabulary." Thank God it was a living voice, a man and not a recording.

"This is Marinda Lawson." She fired her message in staccato bursts. "I've hit a deer. In the car. He's hurt. I think he's dying. I'm so sorry."

"Where are you?"

"Roehampton Gate."

"Where is the deer?"

"Halfway up the hill. On the right. Towards Richmond Gate."

"If you go back and wait there, we'll meet you. What car are you driving? And its registration number, please."

She told them, then retraced the way she had come, though it took longer this time. By now several more cars had stopped beside the red mini and were blocking eastbound traffic; the small stakes lining both sides of the road throughout the park made it impossible to park on the grassy verge.

The deer was still alive, still making frantic, feeble attempts to raise its head. Several people were now standing uncertainly around him.

"Did you -?" the young man began.

Marinda nodded. "They're coming."

Even as she spoke a green Land Rover could be seen

cutting across the grass, avoiding the road entirely, followed by a white police car with "Parks Constabulary" printed on its side. They must have a base right inside the park, she thought irrelevantly. In all there were four men, two uniformed police who immediately began to wave the traffic on, and two gamekeepers in flat caps who approached the deer. These two did not speak but exchanged meaningful glances with each other and then, as if rehearsed, bent and lifted the animal together and staggered with him to the back of the Land Rover where as carefully as possible they slid him inside. Before they raised the tailgate into place, the heaving breathing chest of the deer was clearly visible. So, too, was the small red bubble of blood now dangling from one nostril.

"Will he be all right?" someone asked, but the gamekeepers apparently did not hear as they started the engine and bumped slowly across the grass towards a distant clump of trees.

"Where's Miss Lawson?" one of the constables asked.

"Here," she replied. "I'm Marinda Lawson."

"All right. Everybody else move on, please. There's no stopping here."

Reluctantly they obeyed, retreating to their cars, revving engines, grinding gears. The young man from the red mini hesitated.

"Are you involved in this?" the constable asked.

"No, but -"

"Were you a witness?"

"No, not exactly."

"Do you know the lady?"

"No."

"Then you, too." He gestured with his head towards the road and reluctantly the young man turned to his car with a last questioning look in Marinda's direction.

"Thanks very much," she said automatically as he got into his car and slowly drove away.

"Now exactly what happened?" the constable asked, pen and notebook in hand.

Pictures rose in her mind's eye: a Holbein portrait of Henry VIII followed closely by a wedding photo of her husband, Michael in soft focus - it was strange she had never noticed before how they shared the same thin cruel mouth - but these were pictures she knew instinctively she should conceal, not reveal. "The sun was in my eyes," she answered slowly, thinking that was at least partially true. "I didn't recognize him in time."

"Recognize?" The constable felt a stab of alarm; he had already noted her hesitation and hoped he wasn't going to have a nutcase on his hands.

"As a deer."

"What did you think he was?"

"I don't know. Just a shadow. Perhaps a tree. With the sun I couldn't see that well and I didn't know he was alive until he moved. And then it was too late." She hated lying.

"Is this your car?" When she nodded, he continued, "We'll need to see your driver's license and insurance in the next eight days. You can take them to any police station. Right now we ought to breathalyse you - any objections?"

"No."

"It's just routine." By now he had noticed her trembling hands and was kinder. Nor did his earlier doubt seem justified; she had given an entirely reasonable explanation.

She blew into the white balloon which did not turn green. They told her it was negative. They acknowledged her name and address. They told her yes, she could contact them about the fate of the deer. They told her she was free to go.

And so she went, driving slowly toward the Richmond Gate, knowing they were watching her leave. By now the sun was low in the sky; the park gates would be locked when it set.

I could have told them right there, she thought, right then. I could have shouted, "I'm sorry. I really am. But forget the deer! There's something else at stake, a human life, a might-be murder! And I'm terrified!" But they wouldn't have believed her. The constable had already looked at her oddly when she had said she didn't recognize the deer. She was glad she hadn't spoken about this other thing. They would not have taken her seriously; it would have been not only useless but she would have been guilty of that most English of sins, causing embarrassment.

But the whole thing had somehow cleared her mind, made her think of something else. Once before she had been this frightened, long ago.

* * * * *

A scene from her childhood flashed into mind - as if flicking through TV channels she had stopped, locked on a particular one. Herself as a child. Running. Frightened. Like now. On her way to school. But she had not gone to school, at least not directly; she had made a detour. Into a church.

She knew now exactly what she was going to do and where she was going to go, and was surprised she had not thought of it before. It was important not to waste any more time.

* * * * *

She drove to the speed limit, drove without thinking, without analysing, almost without seeing. She let her fear do the driving, with a purpose at last. A real destination.

Out the Richmond Gate, along the top of Richmond Hill - only the briefest glance to the left where once she would have stopped to admire the breath-taking view below of the lush little valley surrounding the Thames and its tree-filled island. Turner's view, still recognizable, hanging in the Tate. Now a dared glimpse only, a barely-seen ribbon of river turned gold by the dying sun. Then gone, as she turned past the landmark steeple of St Matthias and dipped down the hill past all the little shops and pubs and streets to the white door in Barnes with the curved brass knocker.

She knocked, she rang, she shifted her feet impatiently until the door opened to a startled middle-aged cleric in his shirtsleeves.

"Why, Marinda!"

"Reverend Sam - please may I come in? I've got to talk to you."

The hesitation was too brief to measure. "Of course." But he was obviously surprised as he opened the door wider and she stepped onto the tiled hallway.

"In here." He indicated the study, but she was already through the obviously familiar doorway on the left. "Sit down; I'll just tell Emma to make sure the children don't disturb us."

Returning, he closed the door and looked at her over his half-rimmed glasses. "We didn't have an appointment, did we?" He was 90% certain of the answer.

"No. I'm sorry to come without warning," she answered, twisting her hands. "Oh, and tea-time, too." She managed a guilty smile in concession to his two small children.

"No matter. I take it this is a crisis?"

"Yes."

"Michael drinking again?"

"When does he ever stop?"

"Quite." He began filling his pipe methodically, comfortingly. He waited.

"Murder. I'm afraid of murder." What a relief to say it at last.

The cleric stopped in mid pipe-fill. He raised his eyebrows. "You are serious?"

"Yes."

"Michael?"

She nodded.

He took a measured breath. "I certainly never thought it would come to this. I had no idea." He spoke as if to himself.

"And sooner rather than later. Now, in fact. In fact I was running away this afternoon. Just driving. I didn't dare stay in the house because he was there." She wondered whether to tell him about her accident with the deer and decided against it. It would simply cloud the issue. She looked down at her hands.

"I know Michael has been abusive in the past, but I thought it was verbal. That's serious enough. But you never mentioned physical abuse. Has he threatened you? Has he ever tried to kill you before?

"Oh, Reverend Sam," she looked up swiftly for it was her turn to be surprised now. "I didn't mean - You've got it all wrong. It's me. I'm afraid I'm going to kill him."

II

The Reverend Samuel Sampson regarded his visitor for a moment in silence. Not uncomfortably, for he knew Marinda Lawson well and long experience in the Church had left him virtually unshockable, though still capable of surprise. But he needed time to press both thoughts and words into shape, a need he now disguised through the ritual filling of his pipe, tamping the tobacco down, striking first one match and then another while coaxing the mixture to light. He drew on the pipe several times unsuccessfully, then began all over again, at the same time sending a small silent arrow of thankfulness to the Almighty for blowing out the third match. It was a great shame smoking had become so controversial; it was an invaluable aid in situations like this.

The Reverend Samuel Sampson was an evangelical "low church" man, big-boned and benevolent, his heart truly in heaven and his feet firmly on that part of the Lord's creation - the parish of St Wulfstan's in Barnes - which he considered his own responsibility. Chunky and balding at 46, he was a direct and simple soul who prided himself (while trying not actually to think in terms of the word pride which was a sin, of course) on being as ordinary and as fully human as any member of his congregation. To this effect he proudly (that word again, but he couldn't help feeling it just a little) displayed his plain-but-wholesome and vastly intelligent wife, Emma, at parish meetings and teas, and his two small children whenever possible. He and Emma were a perfectly suited couple, she with her worthwhile part-time job as a social worker (his live-in mother helped look after the children) and he with his equally worthwhile job as the parish priest in one of the most comfortable London boroughs.

It had not always been so, however; his first and second curacies had been served in London's East End where the housing was minimal and the problems maximal. There he had encountered real poverty, joblessness, muggings, two rapes, pub violence, drug abuse, and the aftermath of a non-fatal but extremely bloody stabbing.

So he had welcomed the move to Barnes as a better environment for his new wife and longed-for children, although the ensuing eight years had shown him what he had secretly suspected all along, that the problems here were spiritually the same as in the East End, albeit disguised in the clothing of respectability. He still encountered domestic abuse, for instance - though perhaps done more discreetly, the neighbours being less likely to hear screams, foul language or smashing glass, and the wife far more likely to cover the damage with Estee Lauder make-up on her stiff upper lip the following day. And he still encountered theft - no longer simple muggings but now on the grander scale of fraud and tax evasion. And there were still the sexual sins sometimes overlapping into crimes, the refinement of which sometimes sickened him, a refinement which he had to admit seemed to be in direct proportion to prosperity.

No, he had not managed to move away from the bent imperfect nature of fallen Man. But neither in the East End nor the West End had he yet encountered murder.

Nor was he encountering it now, he reminded himself sternly, peering over his half-glasses at Marinda Lawson. It had not yet happened and with any kind of luck - and

God's help, of course - it wouldn't. He bit firmly into the stem of his pipe with definite intention, then loosened it slightly over the uncertainty of how to proceed.

He respected the woman facing him and knew she was inclined to neither hysterics nor exaggeration. True, she was on the sensitive side and with a lively imagination, but he had put that down to her artistic leanings. He knew she painted - in fact he gathered she had had modest success with that in earlier times, though it seemed to be more of a hobby now. But she was a good mother and certainly a loyal wife. He was more than surprised by this outburst and its obvious sincerity. He had thought of her as a gentle creature above all else.

And attractive. In her mid-forties with her dark hair and rather startling sky-blue eyes, he had always thought she must have been a real cracker at twenty, very near a classic beauty had it not been for the rather widely set eyes, although that in a way merely drew attention to their unusual colour. But there was a sadness about her face which was always there even when she laughed, and which he had automatically attributed to the unhappiness of her marriage. For he had counselled her on that matter, had tried to counsel them both, in fact, although the sessions with Michael, disguised as chess evenings, had become limited as the man's drinking increased, and had finally broken down.

He remembered the unpleasantness of their last evening six months ago in this very room when Michael had faced an inevitable checkmate by standing up, pointing his finger into the Reverend Sam's face and shouting:

"You fucking cheat!"

"No, Michael. I didn't cheat."

He had replied without anger, knowing the outburst was triggered by alcohol as well as the man's profession. Not all actors were inclined to overly dramatize everyday life, but Michael was one of the few who did, behaving forever as if a hidden camera or an invisible audience were in the room. He was a vain man certainly, but not without charm in his better moments. That evening, however, had not been one of them and he had left the house in sullen silence, leaving the Reverend Sam wishing they had not opened the port Michael had brought.

Obviously, he had had a head start drinking at home. But the hidden agenda for the evening had been counselling for the marriage rather than counselling for the drinking, even though he knew the two were closely intertwined. Had he been foolish in matching him glass for glass, in trying to fight fire with fire? Did his own pride come into this somewhere?

He sighed, recognising a moral minefield. And he wondered what on earth could have pushed the slight, pretty woman before him now to the brink of murder.

He knew little about her distant past, just that she had come from Yorkshire, the only child of now dead parents. When he had asked - and was told - that her father had died of silicosis, he knew it was the coal miner's disease, and that that meant a working class background. But if that were the case, the accent had long since faded from the daughter's lips. Perhaps that had happened when she arrived in London to study at the Slade, even before she met Michael.

Certainly she had married well; the Lawsons were Dorset landowners generations back, as respectably inbred as they come. But there had been an estrangement of some sort; the priest knew Michael had no contact with an aging father or a well-known distant cousin, though the estrangement had apparently not extended to finances. Michael had obviously been handsomely provided for somewhere along the line. The priest suspected he had been something of a renegade, abandoning tradition for the precarious life of an actor. Perhaps he had rebelled further by marrying outside his circle, even though he had chosen the attractive and talented girl who had won the Baker prize for painting that year. The Reverend Sam suspected neither that nor her undoubted charisma would have mattered to the Dorset Lawsons.

It was a charisma still recognized at St. Wulfstan's. "She sparkles," someone on the P.C.C. had once remarked. But increasingly it was less so, and certainly not today. It had often struck the vicar as incongruous that the slight pretty woman before him now seemed to have been cast in one of life's tragedies, whereas her effervescent personality should have been bubbling through a light romantic comedy. He sighed again. It was something he might take up with Central Casting when he reached Heaven. Acting was a profession the Reverend Sam had once considered himself.

Suddenly aware that the silence between them had become awkward, he spoke. "Why don't you tell me about it?" he asked, knowing this would give him more time to formulate a plan. "Would you like some tea?"

She hesitated.

"I have the kettle right here." He saw that he had interpreted her reluctance correctly - that she wanted tea but did not want to disturb his family or encourage further delay.

He moved to the small alcove beside the bookcase where a kettle, several mugs and a jar of powdered milk were placed for such a purpose. He often saw parishioners here and sometimes, like now, it was without prior warning. But it was not usually about something so serious, or if it was, it was more straightforward - bereavement counselling or wedding preparations.

He watched as she held the mug gratefully in both hands, savouring the warmth, and smiled for the first time.

"Thanks, Reverend Sam. I really need this since it hasn't exactly been one of my best days. I seem to have killed a deer, bashed my car and thought about killing my husband."

He ignored her attempt at humour, possessing none himself, although he recognized it as a positive sign that her mood was lightening.

"Let's take one thing at a time. Have you really - already - killed something else? A deer, you say?"

She nodded. "At least I think so. I think it's dead. I hit it with the car in Richmond Park."

"Accidentally?" Obviously it was; he wondered why he made it a question.

"Mostly."

He frowned as he realized his question was justified

after all. It was not the answer he wanted nor had expected. Perhaps he did not know this woman after all.

"Mostly?"

"I was thinking about Michael at the time." Henry VIII was an irrelevance she would keep to herself.

"And you wanted to kill Michael." The Reverend Sam was not dim-witted and it did not require a psychiatrist to spot the connection. "But why now? Has he done something in particular? What has happened?"

"I don't know," she answered slowly. "I'm about to lose it, that's all. Control." She did know, of course, what the final incident had been this morning - the lie about the filming in Ireland - but she also knew how trivial it would sound and anyway that wasn't the real reason, it was merely the proverbial straw. How could she possibly distil ten years of goading into a 25-word reason? Michael sneering with his face two inches from her own, Michael silent for days, refusing even to speak the reason for his silence, Michael absent without explanation, Michael present without explanation, and always everywhere the smell of alcohol, wine and brandy, gin and whisky, Michael -

"I know your marriage isn't an easy one," the Reverend Sam prompted sympathetically, "and there's been quite a lot of verbal abuse on Michael's part. (He knew the correct terminology thanks to Emma; it was handy having a wife who was a social worker.) But it hasn't turned into physical abuse, has it?"

Her gaze was locked on distance; he was not even sure she heard him. He wondered suddenly if she was suffering delayed shock from the accident with the deer and he wished he had put sugar in her tea. (His mother had told him that was what they did during the London Blitz when there were so many shocks, so many falling buildings and sudden deaths to cope with.)

"You - and the car - are all right?" He was immediately sorry he had placed the car as an equal concern. She didn't seem to be hurt, but was she? Would the accident explain her behaviour now, explain this whole bizarre talk of murder?

"We're both functioning." Again she smiled, but vacantly, her voice as toneless as if she were answering under hypnosis.

He needed to get her to talk about the situation, about her husband if possible.

"Is Michael still - resting?" He used the profession's own euphemism for being out of work. There were so many actors in Barnes, and more often than not they were "between" shows, "resting", waiting for their agent to telephone or the possible script to clump through the letterbox onto the floor. Even the best of them.

London, theatre capital of the world, where 40 shows of every conceivable description were playing every night in the West End alone, had an enormous pool of talent to draw from, a pool steadily rising and flooding year by year as new graduates streamed out from the nation's drama schools. Small wonder that competition was fierce and frantic, increasingly difficult for the older actor - and Michael, ten years older than his wife, was certainly entering that category. He had been lucky until recently, steadily employed, and while not exactly a household name, was still often recognized in the street. Unemployment, the vicar well knew, brought its own problems regardless of milieu, whether of self-worth or simple finance - though he knew there was family money in the Lawson's case, certainly enough to subsidize the school fees and a reasonably comfortable life style.

"Is Michael still resting?" he repeated.

"Yes, he is." Her voice now had a dream like quality as if she spoke from a long way off and her face was trance-like with exhaustion.

The Reverend Sam shifted uneasily and decided to try another tack.

"How are the children?"

It worked. Her eyes snapped back to the present, to the room they were in.

"They're all right. Heather is spending the night with her best friend, Judy - her mother is collecting them from school, has now already, I suppose," she added, looking at her watch. "And as you know, the younger two boys are safe at boarding school."

Safe was an odd choice of word for boarding school, he thought, but he let it pass. He knew they were there, of course, although not in the same school; Julian was in his A-level year at Harrow while Sebastian, the youngest and brightest of the lot, had made it into Eton where at thirteen he was beginning his first year.

"Septimus? Still enjoying his 'gap' year before university?"

"Didn't I tell you? He's with his friend, Jeremy, seeing America from a Greyhound bus! It's a super deal financially; they've bought a ticket for $99 - that's less than £70 - which lets them go anywhere in the States for

30 days. Julian says the buses travel all night as well and are air conditioned so they're saving on hotel bills that way - though they hate to miss the scenery by travelling at night. So far we've had postcards from New York and Washington and he's wild with enthusiasm." Her face had brightened with the empathy of excitement.

"And Octavian?" He was the eldest of the five Lawson children, out of school, out of university even, and out of the house in a rented flat, training as a barrister in the City.

Her smile faded. "I don't think I've told you - well, it's really only just happened - but he's left law school for a place at RADA. He's decided he wants to be an actor."

The Reverend Sam whistled. "That's new!"

She nodded. "He's always had a flair for acting but Michael discouraged it. You know what an uncertain life it is - hand to mouth between shows, really, and no benefits or pension. Apparently what decided him was a skit they did for somebody's engagement party. Octavian wrote it, acted in it, enjoyed it so much and got such raves from his peers that he did some hard thinking afterwards about careers and what he really wanted out of life. He didn't tell us until RADA accepted him. He's already started - last month, in fact, in September."

"How is Michael taking it?"

"Not very well. He says Octavian's a fool to choose the most precarious of all professions, but there's more to it than that."

"Meaning?"

"Well, I think he feels a little threatened. After all, Octavian is only twenty-two, so very much younger."

"And taller. And better looking. And he may even become a better actor."

"Yes. Michael feels resentful that the Lawson name will open doors for Octavian and that it's his name."

"And how do you feel?"

"Proud of our son. As if we should help him in any way we can. After all, it's Octavian's name, too - we gave it to him."

"In simple terms, Michael is jealous."

"That isn't quite all. There's a money problem, too. Although he's apparently got a grant from RADA itself, it's only for tuition. He'll have to live in the meantime. Michael was giving him an allowance while he was at law school, but he's not prepared to continue if he switches to drama school."

"What about a state grant?"

"No, he already had that for Cambridge. They won't subsidize a second degree."

"Could you fund him yourself?"

She hesitated for a moment, struggling against divided loyalties. "Not really. The only real money I ever had was from the Baker prize and that was just before we got married. Michael invested it rather badly. In fact, he lost most of it for me - us. It didn't matter that much, he had enough for us to live on. But no, he is the only one who can really help Octavian now financially, if he only will. You see, he - Octavian - will have to give up the flat. He can't manage that, even though he's sharing. So he's asked to come home again, just for the three years he'll be at RADA. That, of course, would save an enormous amount, but I'm not even sure Michael will agree to that. He said we would have to discuss it."

Her voice was subdued and a little forlorn. "And you see, there's no time. He's found somebody to take his place in the flat. He's got to move out this weekend. In with us."

"You haven't told Michael that, have you?"

"No."

* * * * *

The Reverend Sam found himself uneasy. He knew he had successfully steered her away from the desperation of her original entrance and that any immediate danger had been dissipated into talk about the mundane problems of a troubled household. But it was a temporary detour; she would most likely be safe - Michael would be safe, he corrected his thinking - when she went home tonight. But what about tomorrow?

Nothing had been resolved; whatever specific cause had driven her to the point of such desperation was sure to return. Even if it didn't, the desperation itself would act as a battering ram and would eventually weaken her other defences through the mere constancy of its presence.

He believed her; he believed her fear. He knew that anyone, given the right circumstances, was capable of anything. And he knew that the unthinkable once thought was easier to think the next time; the unsayable once said was easier to say the second time. Two steps leading to a third, reinforcing it. And the third step was action. Doing it. It was not beyond the realm of possibility that she might actually do it.

* * * * *

He saw his visitor poised now on the second step and he had seldom felt more frustrated or inadequate. It was the kind of situation a social worker would have delighted in, he told himself, it would have been grist for their mill, superb raw material. But she had come to him, a minister, a priest. And in his heart of hearts he felt - not without guilt, remembering that his beloved Emma was a social worker - that that was the right choice. But was he?

True, he still believed, he would still concede, there were different ways of perceiving a problem. He may no longer have believed directly in good and evil - or at least not in evil, Emma having preached too long and loud about the causal effect of genes and environment, but he believed unequivocally that what was facing him now was a moral problem, the possibility, the intention of breaking the 6th Commandment. Thou shalt not kill.

And it was real. That was the problem. A time-bomb waiting to explode, one he had defused only partially and temporarily. In so doing he had had to rely on the crudest of subterfuges, distraction. And not once had he been able to work God into the conversation.

He wasn't even sure how much of a believer Marinda Lawson was. She came to church on Sundays, and on most Sundays Michael accompanied her. Heather, at ten their only child at home, always attended Sunday School. They came to church as a family when the other children were home. But whether this was for appearance or from habit - as he suspected was the case with the majority of his congregation, hankering after the respectable security of a bygone century - or from genuine belief and desire to worship God, he did not know. In a curious way he would have felt it intrusive to ask such a question.

God was a conversational no-go area even for clergymen these days, unless of course they were safely distanced in the pulpit. It wouldn't do to bring Him into everyday conversation, it would be tasteless, thought the Reverend Sam, and even counter-productive as far as winning souls. He preferred to let people know or guess by the simple fact of his profession that God was there. He would never ask if they knew it. They might bring up the subject themselves, he reasoned, and then it would be a different matter. And sometimes they did.

The question he put to Marinda Lawson now was a hopeful compromise.

"Why did you come to me?"

"If you really want to know -" She hesitated. "It's going to sound silly. But a long time ago when I was a schoolgirl in Durham - well, my parents used to take me to church every Sunday. It was what you'd call a low church, no frills."

The Reverend Sam allowed himself a smile. "Like St. Wulfstan's?"

"A lot smaller. But yes. No 'bells and smells'. I don't know if they were believers or not. Almost everybody in the village went; it was the thing to do on Sunday mornings. Then Daddy started to get sick and couldn't go any more. It was hard for him to walk; he couldn't breathe. My mother stayed home on Sundays to nurse him, so of course I stayed, too. I knew he wasn't going to get better. I was afraid he was going to die."

"How old were you then?"

"Ten when he died, but since it took so long I was probably about eight when he more or less became an invalid."

"And when you stopped going to church."

"Yes. I was so terribly afraid he was going to die. Nobody ever said so; they always told him how much better he was looking when they came to see him. But I knew they weren't telling the truth and I was afraid. I can remember running to school every morning and how afraid I was - I thought a big black hairy monster was chasing me and I knew if it caught me it was going to say, "Your father will die!" and that it would be true. So I ran faster all the time."

She gave a wan smile. "I could probably have won a gold medal if anybody had been timing me."

The priest listened, intrigued, wondering where the story could possibly be leading.

"One morning running to school - you know, I can still see the frost on the cobblestones and how white my breath was in the air, making little clouds - I realized I was running past the other church in the village, the Catholic one."

"And?"

"And I could see it was open, not like ours which was only open on Sundays."

The Reverend Sam nodded. He could see now where it was leading.

"So I ran inside. Into a different world. There were candles burning on the altar and a golden cross and at one side of the church there was a statue of the Virgin

Mary all blue and white and gold with a candle flickering in a red glass in front of it. A priest in the most beautiful robe trimmed with green velvet was saying Mass for three people - and there was a rack beside them with three more candles burning, little thin ones. It was like fairyland to me, a magic world."

"I stayed at the very back, just inside the door, trying to be invisible, trying to hold back my breathing which was so loud after running. And I said the first real prayer I'd ever said - not a memorized Prayer Book one, but my very own prayer of petition - that my father would be allowed to live."

"Did that happen?"

"No. He went on dying. But the black monster that was chasing me went away. When I went back outside he was gone and I wasn't afraid any more."

"Did you ever go back?"

"Oh yes, every morning on my way to school. It was my secret. And my strength. My rebellion perhaps."

"Did your parents ever find out?"

"Not until Daddy died. Then the priest came round to see my mother and said how sorry he was and told her that I'd been coming to Mass every morning. I didn't think he'd noticed me - I always arrived just after Mass started and left before it ended and of course I didn't participate; I only stayed at the back and watched. Besides, I didn't think he would know who I was, but I should have known in a village our size he could easily find out. And obviously he had. He told my mother he would like to prepare me for confirmation. Of course she was horrified and refused, and made me promise never to go back."

"And did you?"

"Go back? Well, I meant to - but not for a while, since she was so upset about Daddy dying and everything. But then we had to move - it seems our cottage was tied into Daddy's pension or something. So we went to live with my grandmother in Yorkshire. So no, I never went back. Everything was different in Yorkshire. After awhile I forgot about it completely."

"Church was different in Yorkshire?"

"We just didn't go. I don't know why. Perhaps because my mother was working then. I didn't really go again until I married Michael. He thought we should, that people did."

The Reverend Sam's bushy eyebrows shot up but he said nothing. He was surprised that attending church had been Michael's idea.

"I was happy with that," Marinda continued, "and happy with St. Wulfstan's here. I think I've always been a long-distance believer. But I honestly don't think I've thought about what happened in Durham from that day to this. Then today - it was the same kind of fear, the unimaginable terror of a black monster running behind me - and I remembered. If I'd been back in the Durham village I'd have gone straight back. But I'm not. And so I thought I would come to you. I'm sorry to have told you all this - I know I've gone on far too long about it - but you did ask. I've come to you because I just don't know where else to go," she concluded simply. "And I am so afraid."

The Reverend Sam cleared his throat. He had certainly

got more than he had bargained for with his question, but it had been most enlightening. He understood Marinda Lawson more than he ever had before. Or less. It was very complex and he knew he must be careful. Not for a moment did he underestimate the risk behind her fear.

"So you have come to me - and I'm going to send you to someone else." The decision surprised him almost as much as it obviously surprised her, but a lightning bolt of inspiration had suddenly speared and seared his brain as she was talking. Brother David. Of course. It was an idea just short of the miraculous. Another small arrow of thankfulness - more of a dart this time, really - was fired in the direction of the Almighty.

"Not a doctor?"

"No." He removed his pipe and leaned forward in his chair, pleased by his resolution. "I'm going to send you to one of the Godfathers."

"The what?" Images of black-suited men with white ties and machine guns were obviously flitting before her widened eyes.

"That's the nickname the locals give them. Like the Cowley Fathers - you've heard of them?"

She hadn't.

"No matter. It's a religious order not far from here, a monastery, and I'd like you to see one of the monks there who's a friend of mine. Brother David."

"Oh, but I thought you - " she broke off, confused. "That is -" she stopped again.

"You thought I wasn't into all that "high church" sort

33

of thing," he said matter-of-factly as she nodded, looking faintly embarrassed.

It was a fair enough comment. In taking such care to appear as human as any of his congregation, to be one of them, he had carefully discarded the "Father" image of the Anglo-Catholic priest even to the extent of wearing his dog-collar only on Sundays or for weddings, baptisms and funerals. Not for him the crucifix-brandishing ways of his high church brothers with their incense and confessionals; he had never made any secret of this.

He had accepted the nickname "Reverend" in the way an army chaplain accepted "Padre"; when an East End builder had first used it he was delighted, it meant he was one of them, one of the people (they had nicknames, too) even though it was rather incorrect and he suspected he was the only priest in the Church of England to be called that to his face. He liked it for another reason as well, for it meant he would not be called "Father". And so the nickname had travelled with him to Barnes, where people thought it quaint - and never mistook for a moment his emphatic low churchmanship.

So it was small wonder that Marinda Lawson should be surprised by his reference to a monk. (Even though this was a perfect example of the Church being broad enough to encompass all points of view, as it was continually claiming it did, he decided it was not the right time to point this out.)

"He's an old friend of mine from theological college. Sometimes - not very often, but when somebody has a particular theological stumbling block - which I think you have - I send them to him. Reports coming back are usually excellent. I'll give you his address."

He wrote it down on a slip of paper, rather like a doctor scribbling a prescription.

"Will you promise to phone him today?"

"All right." It was impossible to tell whether she was relieved or disappointed but she took the paper, put it in the pocket of her skirt and rose to go. "Thank you. I'll see myself out."

He nodded, recognizing that small need for independence.

But as she reached the door of the study she turned with her hand on the knob and spoke again. "Just tell me one thing though, Reverend Sam. Just tell me what forgiving is all about. What is it? I want a definition."

He was taken aback, unprepared, for it was a question out of context.

"You need to forgive Michael, is that it? Well, forgetting, I suppose. Not bearing a grudge. Turning the other cheek. Letting it not matter. Making it not matter." He thought afterwards he could have answered better if he had had some warning. It was not a question to be dealt with standing in a doorway.

She looked at him in disbelief, shaking her head. "No, that's not it. But I'd like to find a key if there is one. I don't want to be like this. I don't want to do what I'm afraid of doing, even to be thinking about doing it. I want things to be the way they were. If I could forgive him maybe they could be. But I don't know how because I don't know what forgiveness is."

Her frankness made him remember why he liked her,

and he nodded. "I'll keep you both in my prayers."

Then she was gone, her footsteps receding on the tiles of the hallway.

He put down the pipe which had long since gone out. It had been a difficult hour, but one which he felt had had a vaguely satisfactory resolution. He sighed and stretched. It did not occur to him for a moment that he might simply have passed the buck to someone else.

"Daddy! Daddy!"

"You've missed tea!"

"I've got something to show you!"

"Mummy says to come now!"

The words were shrieked almost unintelligibly together as his small son and daughter, alerted and freed by the sound of the front door closing, came racing into the room, bouncing on and off the furniture with squeals of delight.

He scooped them into his arms. They were a welcome interruption from his many current worries, of which Marinda Lawson was merely the latest. His organist was dying, St. Wulfstan's needed a new roof, and the General Synod was meeting next month to vote on the ordination of women to the priesthood which he strongly opposed. It was October of 1992.

III

"So you're back. Where have you been?"

"Nowhere in particular. Just driving."

"Just driving? Surely you could find something more worthwhile to do with your time than 'just driving'." He leant against the bookcase, glass in hand. "I didn't buy you a car just for 'nowhere in particular' driving." He made an unpleasant mimicry of her voice.

Marinda did not answer because answers depended on what stage he had reached in his drinking. She knew by the first word of the first sentence that it was the beginning of the aggressive stage and therefore silence was safer than repartee. Unless it was a direct question; silence then would be dangerous.

He was making no reference to this morning's confrontation about the filming in Ireland. Perhaps he had forgotten. Or was pretending to forget. Either way it was no time to discuss Octavian's imminent arrival.

She moved to walk past him.

He blocked her move.

"I would like to go upstairs."

"I would like you to stay here."

Until then she had avoided looking straight at him but now their gazes met and locked. His eyes were grey, the whites pale pink - perfect hues for a watercolour ocean sunrise, she thought with bitter irrelevance, alizarin crimson mixed with white.

His expression was triumphant. "I would like you to stay here," he repeated softly, but the invitation was not a pleasant one.

He was a big man. He could stop her if he wanted to.

"I need the bathroom," she said evenly.

"Ah, the perfect excuse," he sneered, stepping aside, watching her mount the stairs.

She made herself climb slowly, even casually, although she wanted to run. Why was she so afraid? This wasn't fear of doing murder, it was fear for her own skin. Yet she knew he wouldn't hit her unless she goaded him, so if physical violence was unlikely why did she feel such physical terror? The handle of the bathroom door beckoned only a few steps away as she turned onto the landing, a big gold knob she had chosen herself. She must not hurry. It was just one more step. Then reaching out her hand she felt all the sudden desperate relief of the medieval fugitive touching sanctuary as she grasped and turned the knob and closed the door behind her.

But she did not lock it. Michael did not allow locked doors in the house, not even for the bathrooms, not even for the children. Had that begun as a genuine safety measure when the children were small, which only later turned into paranoia? She no longer knew. She did know he would respect the closed bathroom door, that he would not enter. At least for awhile.

She remained there a quarter of an hour, as long as she dared. It was the guest bathroom; the fixtures were cream-coloured marble, the fittings gold, and the creamy velvet towels were monogrammed with a golden 'L'. But her mirrored face was white. She splashed water on it for colour, not for the sake of vanity but for the sake of normalcy. Finally she emerged, crossing the landing to the drawing room.

Thick cream-coloured carpets lined every floor in the house, except for the kitchen and the studio. It was a dread-full house, she thought, in the sense that it was full of dread, but it need not have been so. She felt the waste and wrong of it keenly, for it was also a beautiful house. The drawing room occupied the entire front of the first floor, overlooking the Common, just as she was overlooking it now herself as she crossed to the tall windows.

There was still a vestige of sunlight lingering on the highest tops of the trees, or was it only the memory of sunlight? Life or the memory of life? Sometimes, as with the moment of death, it was difficult to tell. High above in the still blue sky a tiny plane caught and flashed like a diamond in the dying sun. And she remembered the deer in the park.

* * * * *

I am pierced with the pain of beauty, she thought fiercely, turning back into the room, awe mixed with anger. For we are surrounded by such beauty that created disharmony is above all else unnecessary, perhaps the greatest sin of all.

The room was filled with flowers and books and on the grand piano a cluster of photographs in silver frames. All five of the children, separately and together, fine looking, tall, big-boned sons in various ages and stages of growth, and at last the longed-for daughter, Heather, she of the golden hair and dimpled chin, adored by her brothers, her father, her mother.

"We will have eight children," Michael had decreed on their honeymoon in that far-off other world they had once inhabited, where husbands ruled like benevolent kings, goodness and justice always prevailed, and happiness was certain forever after.

And so they had christened their first born son Octavian. The idea still held for Septimus three years later, but the enthusiasm had begun to wane three years after that when Marinda, in a rare flash of defiance, had insisted the third son be christened Julian.

They had agreed thereafter to one more child, hoping for a daughter, although it was Sebastian who arrived instead, this cheeky, freckled, brilliant and beloved child, intended last of the Lawsons. For by now they had moved by imperceptible degrees into reality, where colds and quarrels, deadlines and dilemmas dwelt readily and steadily, and Michael had announced that the only problem they did not have - while far from being actually wealthy - was lack of money.

Ah, but it was not true. There were many problems, yes, but in retrospect how small they seemed, how soluble! The sounds in their house had included laughter as well as shouting, Mozart being hammered out on the piano as well as tears and slamming doors. Marinda had knowingly delighted in her children and her painting - in that order - while Michael's career had seemed as sure as an actor's ever can be, as he played the Lyric, the Apollo, the Old Vic, in solid sometimes starring roles with solid sometimes starred reviews.

When he was cast as King Arthur in Camelot at the Haymarket she went to the penultimate dress rehearsal, seeing and agreeing with the popular Martin Gray's portrayal of Lancelot, confidently expecting a strong supportive performance from her husband as Arthur. But from the moment he appeared onstage it was Michael who stunned the audience into silence, bringing a depth of human tragedy to the betrayed king that was astonishing - and almost out of keeping - in a mere nostalgic, whimsical musical. It was a Lear, a Hamlet, leading one critic to label the play itself inadequate for a talent he described as, "a magnificent waterfall thundering into a teacup".

In the final scene where Lancelot and his knights arrived to rescue Guinevere from being burnt at the stake, Arthur the King appeared in a sudden centre stage shaft of light, ready for battle, caught in the gleam of his own armour. Marinda gasped involuntarily as the silver helmet framed his face into an astonishing beauty she had never seen in him before or since.

Afterwards she waited for him on the chaise lounge in his dressing room, sending his dresser away, so that when he entered, smiling and reaching to remove his armour, she shook her head, opening her arms, her heart, and her legs to him. The armour was aluminium; it clanked as he lay beside her but she embraced him and the hard cold metal gladly, wildly, in the wholehearted abandon of romantic love.

And there in full view of the mirror lined with bright clear bulbs and the long shelf covered with tubes and pots of make-up and the costume ermine robe and crown hanging in the corner, their daughter was conceived, by a father wearing a full suit of armour and a mother covered for three weeks afterwards with cuts and bruises she hadn't anticipated. Given those circumstances, she sometimes felt they should have named the baby Aphrodite nine months later, or at the very least, Minerva. But by then the practical world had reasserted itself for good; Heather the child became and Heather she remained. And that had been their farewell visit to Utopia.

(And yet perhaps it hadn't been Utopia after all, not even then, for now, how much later, she remembered an imperfection in that time, in the magic hour when she had lain entwined with her armoured king. For arching in ecstasy, head thrown back and eyes glazed with the haze of love, she had accidentally caught the reflection of their lovemaking in the long bright mirror. She remembered how her heart had surged again at the sight of his magnificent profile in the silver helmet, heaving rhythmically above her, before she realized - with the tiniest grain of surprise even at that moment - that Michael, too, was looking at the reflection of his profile and had turned his face ever so slightly to the right in order to catch his best angle. In the years following she had cut that glimpse out of her memory in the way that we all perhaps edit the past. How odd, she reflected, that it should come back now, years later, unbidden, just that single split-second picture of him looking at himself.)

The Arthur reviews had catapulted him into a kind of stardom for a while - certainly they were responsible for his being asked to join the RSC - although he never again quite managed the excellence he had shown in Camelot. And in a profession where an actor is judged in the main by his last role it began to matter.

The silver Arthurian helmet still sat as a dusty trophy on top of a high bookcase in the study, and one of the silver frames on the piano still held him clad in armour but she could no longer bear to look at it, even less than the wedding photo where the Michael groom standing beside a Marinda bride was quite simply a Michael she could not remember knowing, a tall stranger with his unknown bride.

There were of course other, later, dramatic photographs – in the last he was wearing doublet and hose, holding a skull in his outstretched hand. But there his face had begun to change, coarsened and with thickening jowls, like a wax effigy beginning to melt.

'O what a noble mind is here o'erthrown,' she whispered to herself, 'The courtier's, soldier's, scholar's eye, tongue, sword...' For he had actually been those things, had been 'the glass of fashion and the mould of form,' had had the 'noble and most sovereign reason'; he had had them all, he really had, and her overwhelming sorrow now was more for the loss itself than the emptiness left behind.

She well knew - and was convinced that he knew, too, in his heart of hearts - that his drinking was his downfall. The missed rehearsals and quarrels with directors were matters which spread quickly on the theatrical bush telegraph. In a fit of megalomania he had quit the RSC, convinced he was being deliberately overlooked for the best parts, that he would have better luck going freelance. But it made no difference. Top roles were simply no longer offered; his agent was evasive. He changed agents; that, too, made no difference. This last production of Hamlet had not even made it into the West End, had started and ended at Richmond with a mediocre tour of the provinces in between.

His name still had the echo of a drawing card about it and sometimes - usually, she had to admit - he could still rally himself enough to give an adequate, passable performance. But that is all it was. Had he started drinking because his career was slipping away or was it the other way around? She no longer knew, and by now the problem was so deep-seated it no longer mattered. He had not worked for months.

And he had become a caricature of the man she had loved. The once witty remarks had gradually turned into cruel taunts against her or the children or even strangers; she had once watched in equal humiliation as humiliation was heaped on an inadequate car park attendant. And yet she had clung with closed eyes and gritted teeth to the fact of her marriage vows, frantically redefining love. Until this morning when the astonishing lie about the filming in Ireland had destroyed even the hope of trust between them. He had lied so convincingly, so elaborately, and only accidentally had she stumbled upon the truth. She wished she had not done so.

A sixth sense made her turn now to see him approaching silently across the carpet, two steps away. Instinctively she drew back.

"I didn't hear you, Michael."

"My dear. I was waiting for you to join me downstairs."

"I wasn't coming down." She forced casualness into her voice. Any confrontation at this point in the evening's drinking would have been useless. And dangerous.

"Not even to prepare dinner?" The sarcasm was strong.

"You don't eat dinner. And Heather is away

overnight."

"I see. I am merely to provide, to finance all this -" he waved vaguely at the contents of the room, "but not to partake." Like most professional drinkers he was convinced that if he spoke extremely slowly and carefully the thickness of his tongue would not be noticed.

"Partake of what? Don't be silly, Michael. All this is as much yours as mine." You couldn't argue with a drunk. You couldn't even have an intelligent conversation, she concluded sadly.

"A man has a right to expect dinner in his own home."

"You haven't eaten dinner with us for three years. By your own choice." And how difficult that had been, especially in the beginning, when she had tried to cover for him to Heather and the boys, making little excuses. Daddy is too tired. Daddy has a tummy upset. Daddy is learning his lines and can't be interrupted just now; he'll eat later. All the little pseudo-reasons which fooled no one. They all knew he was in the house, that he wasn't eating because he was drinking. They all tip-toed past whichever room he was in, avoiding confrontation.

But she had confronted him. At first. Dinner is important, she had told him. A family should sit at table together. It was basic. It really mattered. Whatever else he felt or did, he was part of the family. He belonged at the head of the table.

Your cooking is inedible, he had said, so awful I cannot eat it. (Though somehow for the first 15 years of their marriage he had, without complaint and sometimes even with praise.) Your menus are boring.

Perhaps they had become so. Perhaps they really had.

Then tell me what you would like and I'll make it. Give me a menu.

That's not my job, he had said. You should tempt my appetite. But you have no ability, no imagination. What you serve is slop.

I will enrol in a Cordon Bleu cookery course, she had said, swallowing her pain. And did. Perhaps she had after all become complacent, too engrossed in her children, her hobby of painting. It did not help.

You eat too early, he had said. I cannot possibly dine before 8:30. (Knowing that would be too late for the children, thinking she would give up. Any excuse to keep the solitary drinking time inviolate. And unlimited.)

Already he had said the children should eat separately. But she had pointed out that Julian was then 13, Sebastian 10 and Heather 7. They were too old for nursery teas. And when the others were still at home they had eaten as a family. She could not isolate them now, could not serve two separate dinners every day.

That's your problem, he had said. If you want to be a nanny, go ahead. Seven o'clock is too early for me. (Though for the first decade of their marriage it hadn't been; she remembered him leaning through the door of the dining room as she was setting out the food to say, 'Smells wonderful, Mrs. L - can't wait!') But that was long ago.

I cannot possibly dine before eight-thirty, he had repeated years later. For Christ's sake leave me alone. Give it up.

But she hadn't. Then dinner will be at 8:30, she had said, thinking she was doing the right thing. Starting tomorrow. And she had prepared a large sandwich tea for Julian, Sebastian and Heather at 5:00 o'clock so they could last, however tired, until 8:30 (it was at least worth a try, anything to make them a family again; she was glad that Octavian and Septimus had escaped into the outer world of school and university before this had happened). Then remembering the complaint about her cooking (the Cordon Bleu diploma still weeks away), she had nervously driven all the way to the Harrods delicatessen for a game pie, his all-time favourite.

The family had gathered; the table had been festive with its flowers and matching candles (she knew lighting and colour were as important in real life as they were onstage or on canvas) and Michael had come when she called, had sat reluctantly at the head of the table. But the food lay on his plate untouched, cooling before his sullen silence. Nor did he touch the wine she had provided, having left his glass of scotch half full and waiting in the study. He made no eye contact with any of them, but watched their plates with the keenness of a hawk as they ate, as she burbled with nervous false brightness about the inconsequentia of the day, and the children answered her cues in unnatural, overly-cheerful, well-mannered tones.

Sebastian was always the last to finish and his father by then was leaning forward, embarrassingly intent on the boy's plate until he had at last swallowed the final bite. Then Michael had moved swiftly, raising his own right hand high in the air. The children, startled, caught their breaths, waiting. And then he spoke.

"Please, teacher," he had said with elaborate politeness, looking directly at Marinda for the first time, "May I be excused now?"

47

No one spoke as he scraped back his chair and rose. And she had remembered that the word sarcasm was a derivative of the Greek sarcazo, which meant 'to tear flesh'.

She did not ask him to come to the dinner table again. That was over three years ago.

* * * * *

Now the evening pattern was predictable. He would wander about the house drinking steadily until 10:00 or 11:00pm, then walk with only the barest perception of a stagger into the kitchen, place a single slice of bread in the toaster and turn it to the highest setting. While the burning smell unpleasantly pervaded the house he would eat the toast, black and smeared with paté, washed down with wine. Sometimes he would fall asleep on the kitchen chair; otherwise he would drag heavily upstairs and collapse onto the bed, where she would be feigning sleep herself.

"A man has a right to dinner in his own home," he repeated now, ignoring her earlier retort, unaware of his own irrationality.

"Very well." She moved swiftly past him and down the stairs into the kitchen. There was no way she intended to cook a full dinner, knowing it would not be eaten, but she placed a frozen quiche in the oven and began to make a salad. For peace. For compromise. It is what she would have had herself later on a tray while he would have been upstairs drinking. With any luck he would change his mind or forget by the time the quiche was ready.

A conservatory led off the kitchen and through its glass walls she could see the garden, darkening with dusk. The distant drone of planes heading for Heathrow had begun, indicating the evening flight pattern was over their part of Barnes. They were far away comforting sounds, like waves on a shore, rhythmic reminders of an outside world. Of escape even.

She heard a tinkle of music from the study and knew he was refilling his glass. The liquor cupboard was there among the books, a mirrored shrine set in the wall, lighting as the door was opened to reveal an alcoholic Aladdin's cave of glass shelves, coloured decanters and crystal glasses, bottles of every description doubled and trebled by mirrors ad infinitum. No bar could have been better stocked. And it had the unusual feature of an inbuilt music box, triggered along with the light when the door was opened, so that the notes of "Hi Lily, Hi Lo" sounded whenever a drink was being poured.

That had been her idea, to have a song from the favourite film of their courting days installed as a whimsical birthday surprise when they had first moved into the house. And he was pleased. Drinking had not yet become a problem. Later, when it had, he accused her of using the music to monitor his drinking, and he became an expert at holding the catch of the lock with his thumb as he opened the door, pouring a drink with his other hand. That way only one note or half a note escaped, or sometimes none at all. Tonight he didn't seem to care, the entire song tinkled forth. The words were missing but she knew them well.

A song of love is a sad song ...

She couldn't believe she had ever been so naff as to install the thing.

For I've been in love and I know ...

The tinkling stopped and he appeared in the kitchen doorway, glass in hand.

"Why are there so many dirty dishes?" His tone was aggressive and the question made no sense.

"There aren't that many." She spoke lightly, as if humouring a small child. She had used the cutting board for the salad, a knife, the peeler. A small glass bowl for mixing the dressing. This morning's coffee cups were neatly stacked in the sink with Heather's plate and cereal bowl. There was her own bowl from soup at lunchtime. As usual on Thursdays, Michael had lunched at the Garrick. Important for his career, he said, to mix with other actors, directors, producers. He was usually still controlled at lunchtime. And like most theatre wives she was grateful for precious hours on her own.

"I want to know why there are so many dirty dishes!" The tone was now menacing; he took a step closer.

"What do you want me to say? There are dirty dishes because there are dirty dishes. Each one has been used. Each one will be put in the dishwasher later on."

He grabbed her arm. "I want to know why there are so many dirty dishes!" he repeated in fury, driven by fear as he tried to exert the nameless authority he felt should be his, even though he could not remember why.

Her arm hurt; she knew tomorrow there would be a bruise. She jerked it free. "That's a stupid question and you're not making any sense because you're drunk. You're always drunk."

Anger swallowed her own fear in the same way that Concorde swallowed all other sounds twice a day, was swallowing them even now as it flew overhead, leaving the whole land awash and rocking in its massive roar. Conversation was momentarily impossible; she felt exhilarated by the sound, suddenly capable of anything.

Michael's voice was temporarily drowned in the roar of sound though she could see his mouth still framing words, working in silent fury. " - rotten and if I drink it's because of you, you bitch." The words washed up like flotsam on the shore as the roar receded. Left-over words from the shipwreck of a relationship.

She walked past him out of the kitchen, omnipotent in her anger, blind as to direction. She had a momentary urge to hit him over the head with a cricket bat and knew she must not, knew she would not. But she must walk away. Where? Simply away from him. Past the dining room, too open. Into the study, secure, a lair of books. She closed the door, safe again in her own space. He would respect the closed door. He always had.

What if he didn't? All he had to do was turn the doorknob. And then? She needed an inner guarantee of privacy, of safety. Did she dare turn the lock? Her anger now was for herself, that she had ever pandered to such a rule, to such control. Why on earth shouldn't she bolt a door if she wanted to? He would not, need not, even know she was committing the unpardonable sin. The ornate key stood permanently in the antique lock before her. The temptation was overwhelming.

She reached out and turned the key in the door, feeling the lock slot heavily into place, firmly, safely. And loudly. For he heard it, too. Just as she was exhaling the weak triumph of relief there came the first shattering crash on the door. And then another. And another. She realized with horrifying surprise that he was trying to kick the door down.

White paint flew off in uneven flakes. Would it hold? Another jarring crash. His kicks were regular now as a battering ram, with five or six seconds in between each blow. She stood transfixed, stunned by the violence of assault. The door jamb cracked and began to splinter. The door itself was made of oak, thick. But how thick? How long would it hold? And what was he going to do when it gave way? What on earth had she precipitated? She thought of Heather and for the first time gave silent thanks that the little girl was spending the night with her school friend.

The wood shook with another crash and a thin line appeared in the top left panel of the door. Next time it would widen, perhaps give way. She counted the seconds, waiting, braced for the next assault. It didn't come. Had he gone for a tool perhaps, a weapon to make it easier?

Her hands were cold with fear, primitive unreasoning fear which erased the image of a cricket bat, wiping it out completely.

She held her breath, listening, but could hear nothing. If he had gone away, surely she would have heard his footsteps receding, even on the carpet? She took two tentative testing steps of her own and yes, they made a sound, a soft vibration. Then he was still there outside the door. Just standing there. Waiting.

For what? Sooner or later she would have to come out. It was like a siege in the Middle Ages, a mini-siege, his foot was the battering ram. Almost farcical in another context, not here, not now. There was neither food nor water in the study. More importantly, there was no bathroom and he must have figured that out. His higher powers of reason might be clouded and shrouded in an alcoholic haze but he was still capable of basic animal cunning. He would know that she was trapped. The silence now was sinister, almost worse than the smashing, crashing, reverberating kicks.

There was, of course, a window, but its panes were small and leaded and the key to the window itself hung on a rack in the kitchen. Security had been a prime feature of the house when they bought it.

Her eyes swept the room in quiet desperation. All those books were useless now - unless there was one on Great Escapes and she knew there wasn't. There was of course the liquor cabinet - another kind of escape, she thought in bitter irony. How stupid she had been to choose the one room which cut him off from his supply! She simply hadn't thought. He always moved about the house with his glass, but of course the re-fills were here in the study. But she hadn't intended to be in the room for hours on end, as now looked likely. He wasn't totally cut off, she reasoned; there was still the wine cellar, surely he would remember that, even though he preferred grain to grape.

The silence on the other side of the door was frightening, terrifying without definition. A sober Michael, however unpleasant, was at least safe, this Michael, drink-filled and silent, lying in wait, was a sinister stranger.

Again her eyes scanned the room in desperation. The books, the liquor cabinet, two Morris chairs, the desk, the bronze bust of Michael on a plinth in front of the window. Ha! She could have battered her own way out with that, if she had been caught in a different scenario. Was there nothing else to help her, nothing? The impossible window. The locked door. That was really the only way out, that door with its four panels held by a central cross of oak. She was surprised it hadn't given way, and wondered if the whole thing might be carved from a solid piece of wood. But looking more closely she could see that it was not. The panels were separate and thinner, were slotted into the central cross and would surely splinter eventually if he resumed kicking. One panel was already cracked along its entire length. The strength lay in the cross itself which reinforced the panels; it was massively strong, and she knew that part would hold forever.

She had not seen it as a cross before. A Cross. Impulsively she knelt before it and prayed. O great Creator of the universe, I have marked the piercing beauty of this day, and now I am so afraid, afraid for me and afraid for him, because if I had a gun I know what I would do. And it would be self-defence, more than self-defence, a stopping, a peace. Don't let me do that, help me, please get me out of here.

And then embarrassed and unable to concentrate further, she rose and began her survey of the room again. The books. The liquor cabinet. The desk. The telephone.

The telephone! She scarcely breathed as she moved towards it, lifted the receiver and heard the blessed dial tone. She hesitated briefly, reluctant to involve friends, before thinking of the priest she had left earlier. There would be little explaining to do with him.

His wife answered.

"Reverend Sam, please?" she asked in an urgent whisper. Michael must not hear. Suppose he cut the telephone cable?

"I'm afraid he's gone to a meeting." The voice was crisp and efficient.

"Oh, no." A sinking feeling in her stomach.

"Is that Marinda Lawson?"

"Yes."

"Are you all right?" The antennae of the social worker were picking up vibrations.

"Not really."

"What can I do?"

"Please -" she hesitated only briefly. "Could you come to our door? Just ring the doorbell. Ask for me."

The woman asked for no explanation. "I'm on my way."

Thank God for Emma Sampson, Marinda thought, replacing the phone, and thank God for a mother-in-law who lives with them so she can leave the kids at a moment's notice. But awful to have to ask her. Yet she knew with unshakeable certainty that Emma's appearance at the door - anyone from the outside world entering this sordid little one-act play - would bring the curtain down and the house lights up. Sensing an emergency, Emma would surely drive, not walk - unless her husband had taken the car. Five minutes if she drove, twenty if she walked.

* * * * *

With rescue in sight Marinda's fear receded, was

replaced by a giant wave of humiliation which in turn was replaced by anger. Things could not continue this way, as she had tried to tell the Reverend Sam earlier. What was it he had said? Oh yes, go and see some monk, this Brother David. She put her hand in the pocket of her skirt and was surprised to find the slip of paper with the phone number he had given her earlier. Yet why surprised? It had only been less than two hours since he had given it to her.

She looked at her watch. Could one telephone a monastery at 8:00pm? She might as well try; it would at least pass the next few minutes, and now that help was on the way she no longer cared if Michael heard.

But it was an answerphone she got, incongruous according to her idea of a monastery, of stone floors and candles and water drawn from wells. But she left her name and number.

She began to pace the floor, anger rising again. Michael was destroying everything, their home, their marriage, their lives. She stopped accusingly before his bust, set on a plinth in the window for all to see, wanting to pick up the column itself and hit him over the head with it, crush him, stop him. Or to take the bust itself and throw it at him. She placed her hands momentarily on each side of the bronze head. He had commissioned it years earlier from the society sculptor, Enzo Plazzotta, and she had to concede it was handsome, a good likeness of a then good-looking man.

But it was no longer him. If it had been made of wax and set before the window where it was now, the hot sun of a summer's day would have seen it beginning to melt, the cheeks beginning to sag into jowls, the firm mouth softening and running into a sneer, the whole face thickening with coarseness and cruelty as the fine features disappeared, became transformed into something base. And then it would have resembled Michael. Not an alter-self, a Dorian Gray, a Faustian trade-off for youth and beauty, but a true likeness of the man himself, cruelly recognizable. What was left to treasure or admire in this man? What could be left in the end? The man himself was melting, disintegrating into a pool of hardening, dirty wax. Unsalvageable.

She heard the shrill alarm of the doorbell clearly (the liquor cabinet might play music but never on earth would their door have had musical chimes), heard Michael's steps, the door opening, the bright, rehearsed greeting of the vicar's wife.

"Hello, Michael. I know it's a little late, but-"

Marinda wrenched open the study door and moved into the hall just as Emma Sampson was explaining the papers she was holding, something about a church committee her husband had asked Marinda to chair, how it seemed more sensible to drop the papers in person rather than post them since she was passing the door anyway.

Michael could not have been more courteous as he stepped aside.

"Then I'll leave you ladies together," he said.

His talent for regeneration - or acting - was astonishing; no one could possibly have guessed he had drunk more than the one civilized glass which was empty in his hand.

"Of course I understand why you've come," he added

as he retreated in the direction of the now empty study himself, closing the door. And of course he did.

* * * * *

Emma Sampson, a plump figure with short straight hair and horn-rimmed glasses, continued the church-committee charade for a moment longer before lowering her voice.

"Do you want me to stay?"

Marinda shook her head. "It'll be all right now," she said, "but I can't thank you enough."

The woman looked doubtful. Flakes of paint littered the carpet; the damaged door was clearly visible from where she stood in the hallway.

"Is anyone else here?"

"No."

"Would you like to come home with me?"

"No. It's all right." Marinda knew it sounded inadequate but was uncertain how to reassure her without a lengthy explanation. The immediate danger was past.

"Where are you going to sleep tonight?"

"Is that any of -" she bit off her sharp retort as she noticed the worried brown eyes behind the glasses. "Please don't worry. It really is all right now. I just shouldn't have locked a door, that's all. I'll explain more another time."

Emma nodded sympathetically. "Okay. I really do understand. But try to remember there's always a reason for bad behaviour, a cause. I'll tell Sam and I'm sure we can find it. You must be exhausted now, but would you promise me something? That you'll avoid him tonight? Just promise me you won't share a bedroom tonight."

Marinda gave a tired smile. "I will probably do some painting tonight. And my studio is at the top of the house. I sometimes do that."

The vicar's wife nodded, turning to go, then turning back abruptly. "Is something burning?"

"Oh damn!" Marinda cried, running towards the kitchen where smoke was beginning to pour from the charred quiche in the oven.

IV

She did go up to the studio, knowing Michael was in the study, knowing the moment for violence had passed. It had been an attic until ten years ago when they had done one of the loft conversions so much in fashion. Now it was a huge room spanning the full length and width of the house, with a polished hardwood floor and two skylights. These made it the lightest room in the house, full of marvellous, echoing space. She did not turn on the light but even now, in early nightfall, the two large frames of starlight meant she could make out various objects and familiar shapes.

Her canvases were everywhere, stacked against the walls, hanging on the walls, two propped on easels. The faint, agreeable smell of turpentine came from jars holding dozens of brushes on a wooden table, where tubes of oils lay neatly row on row. It was the place in the house where she was most at home. Michael never came up here.

The other end of the long room still counted as storage space and she liked that, too, liked the continuity of family suitcases and sports equipment, the boxes of old photographs and beloved, outgrown toys. She could just manage to trace the dim shape of Pegs (shortened by the children from an unpronounceable Pegasus), the large wooden rocking horse which had been the serial favourite of all five children, standing slightly battered in his red velvet saddle and mane of real horsehair, waiting for them to return - or perhaps for their own children to come and lead him out of retirement.

"Our past and future," Marinda muttered, stroking the horse's head, knowing the boxes and clutter before her, all those things they had stacked and stored and saved, were somehow a futile attempt to escape, unlock, unravel, dissolve the web of time. It would not work. There was no way, no formula, no key. It could not work. Yet there they stayed, these mute possessions, silent markers of their human limitations. Ah yes, it was a perfect place to paint. And perhaps, just perhaps, painting and music and rhyming words came closer than anything else to cracking the code of time.

She flicked on the light switch. Spotlights flooded the room with light, blinding her temporarily. Even though daylight was irreplaceable, increasingly during the past few months she had painted at night, partly to escape being in bed with Michael.

For if she could delay the bedroom until midnight, he would be deep in the unconscious stupor which passed for sleep. Otherwise, unbelievably, he would still roll over on top of her and increasingly impotent, insist on a travesty of love making, his heart making the squeaking, wheezing sound of a bellows while she desperately tried to imagine and pretend, another Michael, another time, tried to imagine ... to pretend ... tried not to cry.

* * * * *

The canvas on the easel before her showed the back of a man's head. He was looking into a double mirror which stood open like a book before him. The two reflections looking back at him bore no resemblance to each other. Good and evil. They were arresting, powerful faces. Unfinished.

She reached for the smock hanging on the back of the

door, put it on, then hesitated briefly before unfolding the single canvas chair propped against the wall. She sat contemplating the picture. She hadn't got it yet, it wasn't right. More depth. More blue for a cast in the eye?

Two hours later she awoke, stiff-necked and cold, surprised that exhaustion had tricked her into sleep. She should never have tried to paint tonight.

The faint, reassuring whisper of a snore met her on the stairs and she knew it was all right to go down to bed, perfectly safe.

It was a king-sized bed in which she could make out the dark outline of her husband on the far edge of his own side, curled into a fetal position, snoring. A faint sickly sweet smell like warm rotting vegetation hung in the room. She had grown used to it now, this smell of his skin. She imagined it as alcohol diluted with sweat but it was not quite that. Alcohol, of course, was on his breath always, recognizably - but this was rather alcohol transmuted, alcohol which had undergone a sea-change before coming through the pores of his skin. It reminded her of the compost heap at the bottom of the garden. He had not always smelled that way.

She remembered once when he had stopped drinking for a month (angered by the doctor's warning after a routine blood test, and "to prove I'm not an alcoholic!") and the smell had gone away after about the third week.

How had he managed not to drink for so long? Probably by seeing the glass of Scotch in his mind's eye, waiting at the end of the long 4-week tunnel, a glass of Scotch glowing and golden, beckoning like the Holy Grail. And he had done it, there was no doubt about that. With the chalice in sight he had made it.

"There, you see!" he had said triumphantly at eight o'clock on the morning of the last day. And by nine she had heard the first notes of "Hi Lily, Hi Lo" tinkling out of the study.

* * * * *

She slept quickly and soundly as always only to be awakened somewhere in the night by the splash of water; she dreamed of rain in the split second of waking, she was swimming upwards, breaking through the surface of consciousness to the sound of rain. Yet it was not rain. It was too near. Too loud. Rain on wood, splashing on wood. She sat up in bed, unable to see in the darkness. Had she dreamed it? No, there it was again, and so very near - in the bedroom, surely! Confused and apprehensive she switched on the bedside light.

A nude Michael stood with his back to her, peeing onto the floor of his open closet.

" For God's sake, Michael, what are you doing?" She leapt out of bed. "Stop it! Get into the bathroom!"

She seized his arm, turning him towards the door. He seemed startled, unfocused; he muttered something she could not understand.

"The bathroom!" she repeated, propelling him physically and unresistingly into it, towards the toilet, before pulling out towels from the cupboard and running back to the closet where a large pool of hot urine lay on the hardwood floor beside his shoes. It took two large bath towels to sop and mop it up and two more to soak up the glasses of cold water she used afterwards.

Working fast in her fury, she carried the lot down two flights of stairs to the washing machine, set the dials and turned it on.

When she returned to the bedroom he was again in bed, asleep or unconscious, though it was another hour before she showered and lay down herself on the farthest edge of her own side, wide-eyed, trying to unclench both her fists and her teeth. The luminous bedside clock read 4:00 am - near the time when his insomnia would rise and drive him from the room anyway. With relief she heard him begin to stir and sometime after that she began to let go herself, falling back into a light and troubled sleep.

* * * * *

The next morning he faced her over coffee, pale but clean-shaven, dressed immaculately in a new brown suit with a red-veined tie; a red handkerchief flared in his breast pocket. She pushed surprise to one side along with the tart observation that the tie matched his bloodshot eyes. Which it did.

"Good morning." It was a forced civility on her part, toneless but necessary, to which he merely gave a curt nod. How was she to communicate with this man? How could she begin to speak about Octavian?

"We need to talk," she said evenly.

"Talk? Why would I want to talk to you?" The pale grey eyes narrowed directly down to her own.

"About last night."

"What about it?"

"It was a new low in our lives. Michael, you need help. You must know that. We need help."

He was silent.

"Surely you must have something to say about it. Even if you just agree we have to do something."

"Just what are you talking about?"

"The study door for a start." For a start. But no, she couldn't mention the closet floor as well, even now she couldn't humiliate him to that extent.

"What about the study door?" He seemed impatient; he had finished his coffee and now stood up, half-turning and annoyed, as if late for an appointment.

"You tried to kick it down last night. Surely you remember that?"

"You bitch. You make up any lie, don't you?"

"Michael, it's true. You know it's true. It can't go on. You've - we've got to have some counselling or something. Won't you at least give AA a try? Won't you at least talk about it?"

"Don't put that label on me," he said with quiet venom. "My problem isn't alcohol, it's you. I used to think your wild accusations were your imagination, but I was wrong. You're not just neurotic. You're insane. By all means get some counselling. You need it. But don't drag me into it and don't expect me to pay for it!"

He shot his wrist out of his sleeve, raising his arm so suddenly she winced, but it was only to look at his Rolex watch. He gave a sardonic sneer at her reflex.

"You see?" he said. "And now you've made me late! Thank you very much!"

He turned on his heel, striding into the hall. For the first time she noticed the small suitcase by the front door.

"Where are you going?" In your new brown designer suit with the red tie and the red handkerchief, where are you going?

"Just a few days away from you, my dear. A well deserved rest."

"In Ireland, I suppose," she muttered dully, remembering the lie about the filming, remembering this was the day he had said he was supposed to go there to film a commercial, before she had discovered it was not true, that there was no commercial. Surely he wasn't going anyway, now that she had found out?

"Not Ireland as it happens," he said with the beginning of a thin cruel smile. "That was merely because I was trying to spare your feelings. A pity you're such a snoop. Otherwise they might have been spared."

He picked up his case and opened the front door. She did not need to see the black taxi, she could hear the percolating sound of its diesel engine and knew it must have been waiting.

* * * * *

Their conversation had been nothing but confrontation, full of hate; there was no moment when she could have mentioned Octavian and his need to move back home over the weekend. Now she would have to make the decision herself - not that it involved a decision. This would always be his home when he needed it. He was their son. Surely Michael remembered that, didn't he? Or did he?

Did he really not remember what had happened last night? Still holding her mug of coffee, she walked along the hall. Or was he pretending not to remember? Her eyes went to the study door, and yes, there it was; she traced her fingers along the hairline crack running all the way down the lower left panel.

Here, you see, she began in imaginary dialogue to her husband, here is the proof that you tried to kick the door down last night.

What proof, you stupid bitch? That crack in the door has been there for years.

Then look at the flakes of paint on the carpet - they haven't been there for years!

But where were they? The carpet was clean. There were no splinters of wood on it, no white flakes of paint. She looked at her watch automatically even though she knew Rosa didn't arrive to clean until 9:30. Michael must have picked them up himself, must have hoovered briefly while she was still asleep in the early hours of morning. Then he had known, had remembered.

Hadn't he? But what if he truly believed what he had said about her making it up? Was truth what she thought had happened or what he thought had happened? If each truly believed a different thing, would the deciding factor be the greater force of belief? Would that have any bearing on the actual fact of what had happened? Was truth so relative after all? Was it possible she herself could be wrong?

She shook her head as a more sinister thought flitted through her mind, bearing the echo of Michael's words. You're not just neurotic. You're insane.

She wandered into the utility room, clutching her cold coffee, looking at the silent washing machine. Yes, there were towels inside; she could see them through the glass porthole of a door, wet and clean, still stuck to the sides from the machine's whirling centrifugal force. But perhaps they were a normal wash she had put in sometime yesterday, not towels she had used in the middle of the night.

Perhaps Michael had not urinated in the closet at all. Or tried to kick the door down. Perhaps none of it had happened. Perhaps their marriage was in trouble because she could no longer distinguish between imagination and reality, could no longer even define reality. Perhaps she really was losing her mind.

V

Rosa, the 'daily', arrived every morning at 9:30 on the dot. She had been late only once in the fifteen years she had worked for the Lawsons and that had been due to a bus strike. Marinda used to wonder whether she arrived in Barnes even earlier, remaining hidden somewhere until she could walk through their door at the precise moment of her appointed time.

In actual fact this was the case; Rosa had initially timed her journey from Acton at 45 minutes, then had added an extra hour on top of it, just because you never knew what traffic was going to be like. Sometimes she got off the bus early, just across Hammersmith Bridge, in order to walk by varying routes to the Lawson house, and sometimes she got off the bus late, at the very boundary of Roehampton, in order to walk back to the house through the woods of the Common.

When the weather was exceptionally bad she would get off in Barnes village itself and go into one of the newsagents, pretending to browse among the newspapers and magazines until her big round Mickey Mouse watch would tell her it was time to go. She looked at it frequently as she approached the house and if she was still a little early, she would stop and pretend to tie her shoe.

Only once - the day of the bus strike - had there not been enough time at all and she had been late, had leapt off the eventual bus at the nearest stop and run flat out for the Lawson house, hair flying, scattering the occasional cat, dog and toddler as she went.

But the residents who had long since recognized her peculiar behaviour also recognized the harmlessness of it, and would usually smile and remark about the weather. As for Rosa, she was thrilled by these casual encounters, since many of them were with the recognizable faces of actors and TV newscasters.

"You'd think I made her punch a time clock," Marinda had remarked once to a neighbour, "but I really don't mind when she arrives as long as she gets the work done."

Rosa Echavaria had come from Madrid fifteen years earlier to live with her brother and his family in Acton. Squat and hairy, unmarried and already thirty, it was the last desperate attempt by her parents to secure a normal life for her - i.e., marriage and children. And since her brother, Juan, earned a comfortable living (by the standards of their remote Spanish village) as a London bus driver, and since his wife was also Spanish and the bond of family therefore strong, they did not object.

Rosa settled easily into their home and was not a burden; she helped with the children and the housework and later contributed part of her wages to the household. In return she received food and shelter, a peripheral sense of belonging - and of course, a free bus pass. But the prospect of finding a husband and a family of her own remained as remote as ever. Although she did find a kind of surrogate family.

Armed with few qualifications of any kind - and even less English - she had initially been taken by her sister-in-law to an agency which specialized in hiring domestic help. And there the name and address of the Lawsons headed the list.

It was the limited fame of Michael Lawson which ensured her work in that household in the first place; although the name meant nothing she couldn't believe her eyes at the interview with his wife - again with Rosa's own sister-in-law present - when Michael Lawson himself walked into the kitchen for a cup of coffee and then walked out again, this face she had once seen in a film in her native Spain. After that they could have offered her any pittance to work for them and she would have accepted.

It did not matter that the remembered film was old and mediocre; it was the first time Rosa had ever seen a celebrity of any kind in the flesh, the first time fantasy had ever brushed against reality in her uneventful life. Had she been younger and born into a different culture, she would undoubtedly have been a 'groupie', following some pop star to gigs at the ends of the earth; as it was, her hero-worship was harmless, if idolatrous, the nearest thing to a divine ecstasy she would ever experience.

She took the job, of course, regarding Marinda and the increasing children as extensions of her hero, and therefore awesome, superior beings. Envy and resentment were simply not part of her nature, she was glad for everything they possessed and experienced in their superior lives and there was never any jealousy whatsoever of Marinda, 3 years her junior. It would never have occurred to her to place herself in a relationship with the Senor Lawson even in a dream; she was content to worship him from afar, to move about his house polishing the furniture he had touched, cleaning the floors he had walked on.

And so the entire family became her possession, her reason for existence; she worked tirelessly and energetically during her half days with them. Her brother and sister-in-law, knowing she was reasonably intelligent, would have liked her to find a better job in due course, say as a hairdresser or shop assistant, which would have carried the possibility of meeting others - hopefully, eligible males - once she had mastered the language. But they eventually shrugged in the face of her obvious happiness with the Lawsons and accepted the inevitable.

Their only hope lay in the fact that she worked mornings only - the Lawsons' stipulation, rather than her own - and that something might happen during the afternoons. But it never did, mainly because she always came straight home after work and did not go out again. She kept busy, of course, by helping her sister-in-law cook or clean or by sewing something for the myriad Lawson children while she watched television. Her understanding of English improved greatly due to the latter, but speaking it remained rudimentary from lack of practice; Juan and Pilar spoke Spanish exclusively at home, while discussion at the Lawsons was necessarily limited to the practical.

This morning as usual she let herself into the Lawson house on the single chime of 9:30 and headed straight into the kitchen for coffee. She always hoped to see some member of the family there, and indeed that is where Marinda would pin instructions on the big cork bulletin board if she herself was going to be out and the normal routine of the day needed to be varied. Otherwise, Rosa would clean one floor of the four-storey house each day, with an overall touch up on Friday.

Today was Thursday, her day for the ground floor. There didn't seem to be anyone else about and the bulletin board held no instructions. Disappointed, Rosa took the hoover out of the cupboard while the kettle boiled. She would carry her mug of coffee about with her as she worked; no waster of time was Rosa.

She began to hoover the hallway carefully and thoroughly, her squat hairy legs planted firmly on each side of the machine, stopping only to attach the long crevice-tool for the corners, watching the bag expand again with its muted roar of sound. This had continued for fifteen minutes when from the corner of her eye she glimpsed Marinda Lawson descending the stairs and her heart gladdened.

"Good morning, Rosa."

"Good morning, Senora." She turned the hoover off.

"What is it?"

The bushy black eyebrows drew together in disapproval. "The door to the study, Senora. Something has happened to it. There is a crack."

Her employer looked startled for a moment, then to Rosa's astonishment gave a huge smile of delight - almost of relief? - and threw her arms around her.

"It's all right, Rosa. It's all right. It was just a small accident last night when something fell against the door. But it's all right. We'll get it fixed. Thank you for reminding me."

Rosa was not sure what she had done to merit such praise but she was pleased. Her employer had never hugged her before and the warmth of such approval was spreading agreeably through her entire body. Still, she was puzzled. It was an unusual household and she couldn't help but notice changes in it from time to time. For one thing the Senora Marinda had been pale lately -

not pregnancy pale, which she well remembered before the birth of the last two children - but pale as if cold, and she had been tense and withdrawn, so that her sudden demonstrativeness now was all the more unusual.

Rosa did not understand but she was worried in some nameless way about her adopted family. She had long been aware of the increasing number of empty liquor bottles in the bin; when the boys were at home she had merely shrugged and felt that young men did such things. But when the young men had gone and the empty bottles had not, in fact their number seemed to be increasing - she found this a disturbing thing, although she would not let herself speculate further. And then there was the matter of Heather's sheets.

As if reading her mind, the Senora spoke.

"We'll need clean sheets on Octavian's bed - he's moving back in this weekend. You'd better leave the rest of the ground floor for now and turn out his room completely."

"Oh, Senora, this is very good! He comes for long?" She liked Octavian.

"Yes, Rosa, a long time. He's going back to school, an acting school. And he'll be living here."

* * * * *

It was a man's voice on the telephone. Unfamiliar.

"Mrs. Lawson?"

"Yes." She was puzzled.

"This is Brother David. You left your number last night."

"Oh - yes, of course I did. Somebody - the Reverend Samuel Sampson, in fact - told me to get in touch with you. I'm sorry it was so late when I called," she gabbled rapidly, not knowing exactly what to say to a monk.

"Let's make an appointment."

They did, for the following day.

VI

Collecting Heather from school was always a bright spot in the afternoon, the small moment when all other demands were put on hold. If Marinda pictured the day as a mass of colour on a canvas - which as an artist she sometimes did - then morning was at the top, just under the frame, coloured according to circumstance or her mood of the day, but the afternoon, in the middle of the lower half of the canvas, would always hold a lightness, a Turner-esque brightness which needed neither outline nor definition. It simply stood for Heather, for the moment of reunion with her youngest child. The bright spot on even the darkest canvas of even the darkest day.

She waited now in the wide tiled hallway with the other mothers, au pairs and nannies, for it was school policy not to release a child until someone was there to collect her. Safety and common sense. But there was also the story of the girl who had simply been left behind, whose mother had forgotten it was the au pair's afternoon off and had carried on with her bridge party until the police finally rang her doorbell. Apocryphal it may have been but the story had had the desired effect on Marinda as well as others; they arrived on time to collect their daughters and charges.

She nodded now to familiar faces and moved a little apart, hoping to discourage conversation. Rows of sky-blue blazers lined the walls on both sides of the hallway at child level. The names were printed in thick black letters on cards above each hook, so large that it was easy to read HEATHER LAWSON halfway down on the left.

Today Marinda would collect Heather's friend, Judy Fisher, as well. They had spent the night together at Judy's house, and it was Judy's brother, Jeremy, who was travelling now with Sebastian in America. The two families had been firm friends until the Fisher father had deserted over a year ago, although Michael had begun to withdraw from mutual gatherings even before that. But Marinda's relationship with Susan remained unaffected, as did the children's. Normally, because of homework, an overnight for Heather would have had to be on a weekend, but because yesterday had been Judy's birthday, they had made an exception.

It now felt as if the little girl had been away much longer than a single night, but once again Marinda gave an inward shudder of thankfulness that she had not been at home. Perhaps it wouldn't have happened if she had been there, the kicking of the study door and all that followed. But perhaps it would have, and even had the child been asleep, the atmosphere of violence and hatred would surely have lingered the next morning and been felt, would have been left stamped on the walls and hovering in the air like spray from a can of poison insecticide. Only when Michael had gone away this morning had it begun to dissipate, so that she felt she could breathe without being sick. Now at least there would be temporary peace. She wished she could know how long it was going to last.

"Mummy!"

The girls all looked the same in their grey skirts, yellow blouses and sky-blue neckties as they poured through the double doors at the end of the hall.

"Mummy!" The girl leapt at her, locking her arms

around her mother's neck in an almost embarrassingly tight embrace.

"Hello, darling." She bent over to unclasp the thin arms and put her down, thinking that a ten-year-old was too heavy to lift for long. "How was school and how was your night at Judy's?"

"It was fun," volunteered Judy, who had come up behind them, struggling into her blazer, eyes solemn behind blue-rimmed glasses.

"I want to go to Judy's again tonight, Mummy, please?"

"No, darling, it's a week night. You know last night was an exception."

"Thank you for my birthday present, Mrs. Lawson, I really loved it."

"Oh please, Mummy, I don't want to go home!"

"Let's wait until Friday and maybe Judy can come to stay with us. Would you like that?"

"No, I wouldn't. I want to go to her house."

"Why, Heather!" It was unlike the child to be so insistent, with obstinacy verging on rudeness. She would try another tack. "Besides, Daddy has gone away filming and that big house will be lonely tonight if you're not there." For the sake of her own integrity she made her tone a jesting one.

The girl looked at her keenly with her long-lashed blue eyes. It was impossible to know what she was thinking.

"How long is Daddy away for?"

"I'm not sure. It could be a few days or it might be

quite a while; it depends on the filming."

"Then I'll come."

By now she had wriggled into her own blazer and the three of them had reached the doorway where the Matron was waiting.

"Goodbye, Mrs. Stock-Lely."

Each girl extended her hand to the Matron's own and dropped the regulation curtsey. Judy was called back.

"Look at me when you curtsey," the Matron admonished. Her grey hair was pulled back into a stern and perfect knot.

The girl did so as she repeated the little bob.

"Now look at me and smile when you curtsey." The tone was fierce, the child complied, Mrs. Stock-Lely relaxed her frown - her eyes meeting Marinda's with just the hint of a smile - and they were released.

The girls piled noisily into the car while Marinda held the phrase, "The Discipline of Manners" in her head as if she were naming a painting.

* * * * *

They dropped Judy at her house, waiting in the car until Susan opened the door, smiling and waving as they drove on. I must ring her later, Marinda thought, after Heather has gone to bed.

Dinner was a picnic on the floor of the drawing room, a custom Marinda had invented long ago for the children on rainy days or for special treats, when Michael really was away filming.

Somehow today qualified for a treat, despite its hazy

autumn sunlight and there being nothing tangible to celebrate - unless it could be the fact that Michael was away. (Away, leaving peace and such relief in his wake and yet also a strange heaviness which lay like a stone in her heart.)

Heather had squealed with delight at the suggestion of a picnic, and had set to work on her homework with great purpose while Marinda made sandwiches and biscuits to fill the big straw hamper. Afterwards they duly carried it upstairs, spreading the red-and-white checkered tablecloth on the carpet where they sat cross-legged, ignoring the French furniture and chandeliers, pretending they were in a forest.

"Mind the ants," Heather warned.

"Oh yes, I will."

"And there are wasps."

"We'll have to be careful about wasps. Sometimes people are allergic to wasp-stings - did you know that?"

Heather nodded wisely. "Of course I know. They have to carry anti-histamine with them." They chewed for a few moments in silence.

"Look at the crows!" Marinda wasn't pretending now; the great floor-length windows of the drawing room overlooked the Common and there right before them in the giant branches of an oak tree several crows were squawking and flapping their wings.

"I hate crows," Heather announced. "They're black and ugly like nightmares."

Marinda frowned. "They're just birds, darling. Not very pretty ones, but you don't have to be afraid of them"

"I hate nightmares, too." The small face was white and anxious.

Marinda was disturbed. "Heather, darling, you can come to me any time you're having a nightmare, you know that. You can just come and wake me up and we'll talk about it."

"No, I can't. Not when Daddy's there."

"Of course you can. It doesn't make any difference whether he's there or not. Or you can call out to me and I'll come to you."

"You wouldn't hear me."

"Yes, I would." Wouldn't she? It was why she had always wanted to sleep with the bedroom door open, so that she could hear a child's cry in the night, even the whisper of a cry. But Michael, who demanded open doors in his house during the day, insisted on their own bedroom door being closed at night. And so it was.

"Anyway, I can't call you while the nightmare's going on because I'm still in it and then when it's gone away it's all over."

"You could still call me then. We could still talk about it." She herself could remember the bitter after-taste of nightmare, when for a moment reality still merged indistinguishable and inseparable from unimaginable terror. She would like to protect her child from that if she could.

"What are your nightmares about?"

Heather did not answer but began to concentrate closely on the bread crumbs which had fallen onto the tablecloth. She licked her fingers and placed them carefully on the crumbs, which stuck to the wet skin. Then even more carefully she lifted her fingers to her mouth to lick off the particles. This process continued until the last crumb was gone.

"You know, I have something really nice to tell you," Marinda said.

"What is it?" The girl shrugged and did not look up.

"It's a lovely surprise. Something you're going to like very much."

The child raised her eyes now with a flicker of interest, like the unexpected flash of a fin near the surface of still blue water. Ah, for an easel! But who could ever capture such a thing?

"What is it then?"

"Guess who's coming this weekend?"

The girl shrank back into a smaller version of herself, her eyes on the floor as she whispered almost inaudibly, "Daddy."

Again Marinda was disturbed. Had Michael's drinking alienated his youngest child that much?

"No, darling. Well, he might be coming, too, but that's not the surprise. The surprise is that Octavian is coming!"

It was as if she had switched on Christmas tree lights.

"Octavian? Oh Mummy, how wonderful! For how long? Oh, how wonderful! How super-duper fabby-dabby wonderful!" She jumped up and began to dance around the room in movements of pure joy.

Marinda leaned back on one elbow smiling as she watched, knowing Heather loved her eldest brother and had missed him greatly. In fact she loved all her brothers and had had to watch them go away, however temporarily, one by one.

When Sebastian had left for Eton two weeks ago this little sister must have felt the emptiness of the house as much as she herself did. Perhaps it was that which was making her so withdrawn these days, which had made her want to go home from school today with Judy Fisher. Perhaps it was that which made her shrink from the mention of Michael and not his morose and moody drinking. Perhaps.

VII

The next morning she was back in Richmond Park driving the same road she had driven Wednesday afternoon. With what a difference!

For then she had been beyond the breaking point of fear, a glass woman shattered into panic, with sharp slivers of pain cutting in all directions like Picasso's portrait of the Weeping Woman. Now it was as if the fragile broken pieces had been collected and somehow stuck back together, haphazardly perhaps and not quite in place, but nevertheless together. And whatever the glue was it was holding, at least temporarily.

The car had automatic transmission and she drove easily, controlling the steering wheel with the mere tips of her fingers. This morning she was in equal effortless control of herself. Why so, when her situation had not really changed since Wednesday?

Perhaps it was only because Michael was away. Or because she had spent some quality time last night with one of her children. Because she had had two cups of strong coffee for breakfast this morning. Because she was driving now with a definite purpose, a destination, unlike Wednesday. Because going to a monastery to visit a monk was an adventure in itself, one which still carried a childlike excitement and wonder in spite of the century. Because somehow there was hope involved, however remote and indefinable. Because hope was the difference between youth and age, between morning and afternoon, and this was still morning. Because more than anything else the angle of light just now in

Richmond Park was all these things, the hope and joy of all creation compressed into the slant of sunlight.

"The whole meaning of the universe," she whispered to the car, her confidant, "is in the way the light shines." She had never quite been able to capture it on canvas but she had never given up trying.

Passing the spot where she had hit the deer she felt a twinge of sadness. She had not telephoned to learn its fate. She knew.

Nor did she exit this time at Richmond Gate, but continued along the edge of the park on the road she had not taken the day before yesterday. There was little traffic. A single rider cantered silently into the distance but there were no other people; she might have been on a vast country estate instead of driving in London itself. The trees were glazed with gold, their bottom branches trimmed with mathematical precision by the deer to the height they could reach when standing on their hind legs. But just now there were no deer in sight.

She drove on, watching now for the sign to Ham Gate, seeing it soon in the hollow of a grassy dip, a green pointer on a post topped by a golden crown. There were several other pointers on the pole and she smiled at the unreality of the picture, thinking the whole thing could be an illustration from a fairy tale, even though she knew the crown was not a mark of fantasy but an indication of the park's royal patronage - and could see the second arrow pointed to "The Isabella Plantation" and not to "The Giant's Castle".

She turned right, down the long sloping approach to Ham Gate, then through it, past the once-charming gatehouse which had been transformed into a walled and armoured compound by an absent Sultan of Brunei.

Ha! she thought, driving past it, that's every bit as good as a giant's castle or an ogre's den and I could be in a fairy tale after all. But remembering the stricken deer she quickly reined in her thoughts, not wanting to, refusing to blur the boundaries of reality again. She would concentrate on the road itself.

Once outside the gate she was in unfamiliar territory though she had copied Brother David's directions carefully onto a scrap of paper.

The road lay straight ahead through a mile of mini-forest. And sure enough, there at the end of it she could see the single traffic light indicating the boundary of the village of Ham. It was glowing now like a fat red ruby among the trees and she braked slowly, noting with delight another traffic light a few feet to her left, a traffic light on a very high pole, glowing equally bright with the image of a red horse on the light itself. Her directions had not mentioned this. Looking carefully, she could make out the outline of a bridle path leading up to it and then away from it on the other side of the road.

"A traffic light for horses!" she laughed aloud, and as the sense of unreality continued, whispered to herself, "Damn it, I am in a fairy tale!"

Both lights turned green at once and Marinda drove across the intersecting road. Now she was edging a large open field with a small pond in its centre, big old houses set back in the distance, and a sign set into a low stone wall nearby which spelt out HAM COMMON.

"Then this is it," Marinda breathed, surprised that a common could be so open and so small, at least compared to the one she knew so well in Barnes. But this was definitely it. The monastery was right here. It had to be behind the high wall on her right, brick-blackened with age. There was neither a number nor a sign to indicate that she was right, but it couldn't really be anywhere else. Brother David had said the gates would be open and so they were, old wooden gates with a rusty iron ring for a handle.

Carefully she nosed the car through the opening onto a gravelled front garden dominated by the largest oak tree she had ever seen. She parked beneath it. She could not have parked anywhere else since its branches covered the entire garden. That would explain the gravel, too; flower beds and lawn would have been impossible in so much shade.

She was facing a two-storey brick house, probably eighteenth century, with later additions. Certainly a conservatory had been added to the front. She made her way towards the greenery of this and the only door she could see, her feet scrunching across the gravel. Halfway there she stopped in surprise.

A crude stone bird bath had been set into the gravel at ground level, and cemented onto it, equally crudely, was an elegant little bronze statue, an unmistakeable Tony Renouf. How on earth did it come to be here? Weren't monks bound to a vow of poverty? She circled the sculpture admiringly, bending closer to look for the signature mark which would validate her guess. And there it was. Of course. Only Renouf would have created a statue of a laughing St. Francis, his robe swirling as he reached playfully to the back of his neck to extricate the dove which had flown into the folds of his cowl. The whole thing was as charming as it was unexpected.

She was still smiling as she rang the doorbell to receive her second agreeable surprise of the day.

For it was opened by the young man she had met in the park, who had stopped his car when she had hit the deer. Only now instead of jeans and T-shirt, he was wearing a black cotton habit and sandals.

The surprise of recognition swept over his face, quickly followed by tentative pleasure. Hesitantly he put out his hand.

"Hi, I'm Brother Thaddeus."

"Good morning. I'm Marinda Lawson - with an appointment to see Brother David."

"I know. But I didn't know it was you. Brother David just said a visitor. Please come in. He said to tell you he'd be with you very soon."

"I think I'm a bit early."

"Yes." He drew in his breath anxiously as if he would say something further, then seemed to change his mind.

And again she was reminded, as she had been in the park, of her son Octavian. "You look very different from our last meeting," she ventured gently.

He grinned, and she felt she had judged his hesitation correctly for he seemed relieved that she had mentioned their meeting.

"Yes, well - we're allowed to wear mufti when we do the food shopping and it was my turn for Sainsbury's."

Then they didn't grow their own food in the fields, she thought in silent disappointment. Aloud she said, "I hope I didn't make you too late. You were really such a help."

"Are you okay?" His concern was genuine and she was touched.

"Of course I am. I just wish I could say the same for the poor deer. It must have died, though I didn't phone to find out for sure."

"I did," he said quietly.

And the sudden sorrow in the blue eyes both surprised and made her profoundly grateful that the creature's death had somehow been noted, had been mourned. By a professional.

They stood in awkward silence for a moment and then he indicated the conservatory with a sweep of his hand. "Would you like to sit down? There are some chairs among the plants if we can find them."

"All right." Then feeling more was required of her she added, "It's very nice," although the conservatory seemed to have nothing but red geraniums in it. Still, they were very large and blooming profusely.

"It's Brother Aidan's pride and joy."

"You have something else to be proud of - that Renouf statue in the garden."

"Oh, yeh," his adam's apple went up and down as he laughed the laugh of a very young man. "Our St. Francis. Wrong on several counts and we know it. It makes us look like Franciscans when we're not, and second, it is valuable and we know that, too. It was a gift, though. This bloke insisted."

"Renouf?" She was prepared to be impressed.

"No, just somebody we helped for awhile. It was his, but he wanted us to have it. He set it in all by himself and he made the bird pool - that was after we asked him to keep it outside the house - because that way we figure it doesn't really count as a possession. Everybody can appreciate it and it isn't really ours. The visitors seem to like it a lot. But it's really 'for the birds'." He laughed merrily at his joke.

She was struck by the easy simplicity - superficiality? – of his emotions and how quickly he had passed from sorrow for the deer to this laughter.

"Anyway," he said with finality, "we're not allowed to be proud of things."

"But didn't you just tell me these flowers were the pride and joy of one of your brothers?" She wished she had not said it.

He hesitated. "Flowers aren't a possession," he said simply. And then slowly, "But I shouldn't have said pride. That was wrong of me. I should have said joy. Brother Aidan takes joy in them." And he smiled so disarmingly with his large buck teeth that Marinda was ashamed she had challenged him.

"The chapel is through that door," he continued, indicating an arch in the corner. "You can wait in there if you'd rather. I'm afraid I have to go back, but Brother David really won't be long." He smiled again before retreating, his leather sandals clacking on the white linoleum tiles.

She stood uncertainly for a moment beside a white wooden chair, then moved through the geraniums to the chapel door. It pushed open easily. She stood with her hand on the handle, peering inside.

It was not quite what she had expected, a simple

room, stone benches which could have seated perhaps fifty, a stone altar. Apart from the crucifix on the altar - also carved in stone - there was no decoration of any kind. Three arched windows at the side held plain opaque glass; she could make out the shape of vine leaves pressed against the glass outside. These must be what were giving the chapel its cool greenish tinge, an almost underwater kind of light.

She shivered in the chill. Without warning an eerie sense of her Durham childhood, dormant and distanced for years, began to settle over her again, the memory of watching the forbidden Mass in an ice cold church where her breath made a ghostly cloud in the air and the only warmth, or thought of it, came from the little candles of prayer on the wrought iron stand before her and the magic candle burning before the Blessed Sacrament. It had been enough; she could still remember the hushed awe which enveloped her like a cloak even as she shivered. She shivered again now at the memory and wondered why it had come back in such a dissimilar place, the third time in as many days.

It was odd there was no host reserved here, no pyx of any kind, no candle burning to indicate the Divine Presence. She glanced at the altar again to make certain. It was not what she would have expected in a monastery. Certainly not what she had found all those years ago in the little Catholic church in Durham.

There seemed to be another door at the rear of the chapel, which she thought probably led back into the front garden and driveway. It would do no harm to see if she was right. With a quick glance over her shoulder to make sure Brother David was not tripping through the geraniums, she stepped fully into the chapel - and heard the door behind her swing shut with an ominous click.

"Oh, damn! Damn, damn, damn!" Then a miniscule breath of guilt, even though she told herself that swearing in a chapel was surely a very minor sin, perhaps merely a misdemeanour, but definitely not good manners. "Sorry, God," she muttered as she re-tried the door to confirm the fact that it had indeed locked itself behind her.

Perhaps for a purpose? She remembered the running child in Durham, her long lost self, and was aware of a fleeting obligation towards prayer, towards meditation, towards at least composing herself. She rejected them all. I'll pray later, she thought; I'm too upset now to even think about being calm. Perhaps, she thought sardonically, this is the monks' way of recruiting.

"Or maybe this is what they mean by being enclosed," she muttered aloud in humour born of panic at the thought that she was locked inside the chapel.

But of course she wasn't. The door at the rear was unlocked and opened easily onto the gravel of the front entrance, just as she had previously suspected. There was the giant oak tree, there was her car, and there was the little statue of the laughing St. Francis.

The door through which she had now come was half hidden by vines, as was the sign beside it where weather-beaten letters announced the times of services:

Mattins	-	7:00
Mass	-	7:30
Terce	-	9:45
Sext	-	12:45

Evensong - 18:30

Compline - 21:30

Did anyone actually come to these? They must, since the times were posted. And Brother Thaddeus had referred to visitors seeing the statue. That must be the reason why the outside chapel door was left unlocked. And that would also explain the automatic lock on the other, inner door. Because people - the great unwashed public of whom she was one, she reflected - could not really be trusted. They might otherwise sneak into the monastery itself, disrupting prayer and grabbing various articles with avaricious hands. Perhaps they already had and that was why the chapel was so bare. Perhaps it had once held stained glass, gold leaf and jewel-encrusted crosses. And candles.

She sighed and shook herself back into immediacy. It was an embarrassing situation and escape loomed tantalizingly near. There was really nothing to stop her driving away again at this very moment. She was outside and her car was right in front of her. But a shadow of yesterday's fear dipped over her and she remembered the real reason why she had come. Why the Reverend Sam had sent her. All the earlier hope and faux lightness of spirit she had felt on her way through the park this morning drained away, and she knew there was nothing else to do now but return to the door of the conservatory and ring the bell again.

Disconsolately she scrunched back across the gravel, wondering how Brother Thaddeus was going to feel about having his morning interrupted a second time.

But it was not Brother Thaddeus who came. After a four-minute wait a stooped old man in black habit answered the door. His hair was a massive tangle of white and his white eyebrows grew together in the middle so that she was reminded of a small furry animal.

"Brother David?" she asked tentatively.

He shook his head. As she began explaining he motioned her inside, and when she had finished apologising he merely nodded and then with a quavering blue-veined hand indicated a chair.

"Thank you," she said, sitting down firmly. "I'll stay put this time."

Again he nodded. Had he taken a vow of silence?

But as he turned away his voice was wafted back to her, faint and dry but not unkind.

"It happens."

Watching the retreating shuffle she understood the four-minute wait outside the door, and had a clairvoyant certainty that she was observing Brother Aidan, he of the flourishing geraniums.

VIII

At last Brother David. Too tall. Too aware. An instant impression of guarded strength; she fought down the image of a Miltonic warrior-angel from the dawn of creation. Was he old? Young? He could have been equally thirty-five or fifty-five. Perhaps he was both, with his asymmetrical bony face; surely normal criteria did not apply to this figure whose shoulders were so broad, whose habit seemed to hang from a wire frame, whose face had the same fierceness she had once seen in a giant mosaic face of Christ in the apse of a Russian cathedral.

She followed him up the stairs; he had said, "I'll lead."

She watched the feet ahead of her. The robe ended above his ankles. Unlike Brother Thaddeus he was wearing socks with his sandals, black socks. The steps were stone, lower than usual; it was an easy climb. Books everywhere in bookcases along the stairs.

Then into a small room, a plain glazed window and two wooden chairs. A crucifix on the wall. Nothing else. He motioned to one chair and straddled the other backwards, folding his arms along the dark wood. She sat, too, her handbag on the floor, her hands in the pockets of her skirt.

His eyes were nearly black. Direct. Waiting. In no way was he what she had expected, although she didn't know what that had been. It was uncomfortable. She herself was uncomfortable, facing this stranger who seemed so very strange. And who was a man. She was conscious of an overwhelming asexual masculinity, so very different from the Reverend Sam's simple manhood. It was certainly no time for small talk.

She cleared her throat. "Did Reverend Sam phone you?" she began hopefully, annoyed that her voice should sound uncharacteristically high, so timidly uncertain.

"No. You said he told you to see me."

She could not imagine the two of them as friends; their difference was indescribable, incalculable. "I don't really know what I'm doing here in a monastery," she began defensively. "I've already been to see Reverend Sam and I'm not exactly wildly religious."

"Steady on," he grinned. "We're not asking you to join the order."

His sense of humour astonished her, erased the awe she had placed around him, replaced it with instant humanity. But he said nothing more as she floundered mentally, uncertain how to proceed before the intensity of his stare. Hell, it was going to be like jumping into an icy swimming pool. She closed her eyes and plunged.

"Okay, I'm not wildly religious but I suppose I am rather desperate. I'll try to be brief." My life in twenty-five words or less, she thought grimly, wishing she could proffer a painting instead, one of those enormous Victorian canvases to depict herself on a hilltop of desperation, arms stretched up to the heavens (serenest moonstone blue deepening to cobalt) while below her in the valley, dark and barely discernible, would be the dead body of Michael (indistinguishable from King Henry VIII), the light glinting on the handle of the silver sword protruding from his chest.

"I really will try to be brief," she repeated, more to

herself than him. She drew a long breath. "I'm married with five kids, age 22 to 10. My husband's an actor. And an alcoholic. He's destroying our marriage, our family. Our lives. I can see it happening but I don't know how to stop him and I don't know how to forgive him. And I'm afraid I'm going to kill him." There. That was it in a nutshell.

She sighed in relief, sat back and waited - for what? A solution? A miracle? Brother David was silent, still watching her intently. Should she say more?

"I know I'll go to prison if I do, and that would be hard on the family, too."

"That's one reason for not doing it."

"I don't want to do it. I'm not - well, planning it. It's just -" How could she explain the pressure, the fear? "I don't intend it. I'm just afraid I will, really afraid when things get unbearable that I'll snap." It sounded like such an excuse.

"Why are you afraid?"

What a strange question. She would have thought the answer was obvious. "Well, I suppose of hurting the children. Of course. But not afraid of prison itself, not of breaking the law, man's law. It's more than that. It's wrong, that's all, on a much deeper level. I know it's wrong. I don't want to do something that wrong. I don't want to break God's law."

With a rush of surprise she suddenly realized she had hit on the truth - although she hadn't known it until she said it. That was what had been at the dark edge of her fear all along, weighting it down, the stone thrown into the black pool of creation, with ramifications spreading like circles throughout eternity. Thou shalt not kill. What really happened when you broke one of the primal laws of the universe?

"Though both man's law and God's law really say the same thing, don't they?" she continued. "Thou shalt not kill."

"Razach. The actual translation from the Hebrew, "the monk said softly, "is 'Thou shalt do no murder.'"

"Define murder."

"You define it."

"Well, it's really only one type of killing, isn't it? The law - or commandment - doesn't refer to execution - or self-defence, does it?"

"And it's those you are considering?" Perhaps she only imagined the hint of a smile at his question.

"Not exactly. No." She spoke defensively now. "I'm not looking for an excuse through semantics, you know. I don't want it to happen at all. I don't want to think about it, to break it down, classify it, define it."

"And yet you are."

It was true. It was she who had queried the definition of murder. "You're right," she said slowly, confused.

His eyes flickered in surprised approval at her admission. "You mentioned self-defence. Would that be likely?"

"No." Michael had never threatened her, she had to admit that. She could not imagine his bloodshot eyes above a gun aimed in her direction; no, he simply wasn't capable of that kind of violence. He had never beaten nor kicked - her racing mind stopped as she remembered the splintering study door the night before last. If the door had yielded, what would he have done? And she? What would she have done? Surely she had been too crazed with fear herself at that point to do anything other than attempt to escape; if the door had given way and he had burst through the splintered wood, she would not have been capable of stopping him, would have had no way of stopping him.

Unless she had had a gun. But they had no guns. She had not thought in such practical terms before. How different it all was when viewed from this safe distance. She could not have stopped him physically, but perhaps she wouldn't have needed to, perhaps she would only have needed to stop the bullets of his words. For those were lethal, too, she reflected, aimed with deadly accuracy, intended to destroy.

"Although there was an incident on Wednesday," she began haltingly, "when I was locked in a room. He was trying to get in and I was very afraid. Perhaps if I had had a weapon then..." her voice trailed off. "But I didn't."

"What did you do?"

"Nothing. Oh well, I did pray." It startled her that she remembered that, her frantic little flare for help, lit and fired skyward.

"And?"

"Nothing happened, of course. But I didn't really expect St Gabriel to come down the chimney with a flaming sword."

"How did the situation resolve itself?"

"I remembered the telephone. I called someone who

came."

"And you see no connection between the prayer and the telephone?"

"How could there be? The phone was already there. Always there."

He smiled disarmingly but said nothing.

"So self-defence wasn't really necessary," she finished lamely, "and I don't think it will be again. That was pretty much a one-off situation." For some reason she felt ashamed.

"Self-defence possibly, but not likely," Brother David continued, indicating her new confusion had not been lost on him. "You also mentioned execution. Which implies planning." His tone did not lift into a question but his eyebrows did.

"You're right again," she agreed. "And since I'm not actually planning to kill him, execution is out." It was all beginning to sound rather silly. Feeble. And yet -

He nodded. "Consider this. If the Hebrew word razach in the 6th Commandment meant destroy, 'Thou shalt not destroy', would that change anything for you?"

"But I already told you - it's Michael who is destroying us, gradually and daily, our whole family. Oh, Brother David, there are so many things in life we can't help - illness and death, accidents and the natural loss of all things through age and time. These are things we can't control and they bring suffering enough. It's terrible to add to them deliberately, to manufacture unnecessary pain. And Michael is doing that."

"All by himself? Are you so innocent?"

"Yes." She met his eyes in defiant certainty. "There is terrible destruction. I only want to stop it."

Brother David's eyebrows raised again. "Let me get this straight. You are proposing destruction to end destruction? As a means to an end. I see."

So did she, now that he had pointed it out, the contradiction in terms, the dichotomy of similarity her action would bring to Michael's own. For her way, however reluctant, however feared, would equally destroy them. She must have known that all along and had been running from it as hard as she could. "Either way there will be no family," she acknowledged bleakly. "If I lose my cool and kill him."

"And no Michael," the monk said. "Do you care about that?"

"I care." Somewhere in a dusty cinema in the back of her mind, an old film began to unwind in black and white. She could see the far off image of a man walking along a summer pathway by a river, a young Michael with his head thrown back, his laughing face unblemished through the soft-focus of her tears. He was throwing a ball to a child who caught it, then another child - smaller - was throwing it back. She recognized Octavian and Septimus as little boys and they were laughing, too, although there was no sound. It was a silent film.

"But he isn't really there any more," she whispered softly, as the picture reel faded and creaked and ground to a halt. "That Michael went away a long time ago. If he ever came back - if he could - for a long time I used to pray he would, that he would be the way he used to be ..." It was true. She hadn't remembered until now, but it had once been a daily prayer for weeks on end. For months. For several years even, until the dull recognition of reality had finally seeped into her acceptance and she had stopped praying. Perhaps she was religious after all. She had forgotten she had once had a pattern of prayer - or at least of petition.

"I have never understood," she said now, "why change only seems to flow in one direction. Why, if people change in some way, it is not possible for them to change back again. Like the Thames. It flows impossibly fast and strong to the sea. Then the tide comes in and - have you ever seen it just at the point of change where the pull is so strong both ways that the water sort of boils and roils in a kind of raging impasse? It's a real battle. But in the end it starts to go the other way, all that fierce current, brimful to the banks, really does change and begin to flow in the opposite direction, right back to the way it went before. It can happen. Is it wrong to pray for that in a human being?"

"Of course it can happen. But be warned about prayer. Don't ever ask for anything you're not prepared to receive."

"Well, of course." What an odd and obvious thing to say.

"Yes, the Thames changes. But remember it changes back again - and then again. Would you have settled for that?"

"Of course not. Though it would have been better than not changing at all. There would have been hope."

"Hope for the past but not the future. Or hope that the past would become the future." The monk seemed to be musing to himself and for a time there was silence between them. It was not an awkward silence nor an empty one. Each was thinking. Finally Brother David spoke again.

"I'm neither a barrister nor a psychiatrist," he said. "I can only see your problem from the eternal perspective. But I am struck by two things. The first is that you have not mentioned divorce. A barrister would probably ask why you don't consider that a better option than murder. Couples divorce all the time. They don't kill each other that often."

"Would you divorce? If you were married?"

The surprise was plain on his face as he drew in his breath in sharp disapproval, then exhaled slowly as if deciding whether to answer. Finally he shrugged. "For me it wouldn't be an option."

"Nor is it for me. Am I the only person in the world regarding the marriage vows as truly binding?"

"I take it you have tried other avenues - marriage counselling, Alcoholics Anonymous, your doctor?"

"It's funny you should mention those. I've suggested them all in the past, but Michael wouldn't consider any of them. He says his only problem is me. And of course," she gave a wry smile, "I feel the same way. Why would I go to AA or Marriage Guidance when the problem is him and he won't go with me?"

Brother David shook his head. "So you are left with me and the eternal perspective. Okay." Again there was a silence, then, "The other thing which struck me was your saying you didn't know how to forgive him."

"I know that's the key. If I could just forgive him then I wouldn't have to be afraid of killing him."

"Then you want to forgive him for your own sake, not his."

Startled, she replied, "Well - both." Then more uncertainly, "Maybe I am putting myself first. I thought if I could forgive him, I could just hang in there and wait ..."

"For the tide to change?"

"I don't know. Yes, that's what I want. For him to stop drinking. For him to change back, I suppose. Anyway, that's academic. I can't forgive him because I don't know what forgiveness really is. People are always talking about it, but when you come right down to it, what is it?"

The monk was silent.

"I keep asking but I don't ever get a workable definition. The Reverend Sam told me it was forgetting, not thinking about it, not letting something matter, turning the other cheek. But that's not it. It can't be that. Unless forgiving comes in tiers -"

"Forgiving always comes with tears," the monk inserted softly, as if to himself, "even though they may not always show."

" - like layers," she continued, "a lower tier for the things it is possible to forget because they really don't matter very much, like a lover's quarrel or cross words between neighbours over the back fence, something that's over. But what's happening to my family isn't over, it's ongoing and it does matter. I can't forget it, not while it goes on happening. Am I supposed to pretend it's not? I've run out of cheeks to turn. And even if I knew what forgiveness was, how could I forgive somebody who doesn't want to be forgiven? How ca-"

Brother David raised his hand palm outwards, the

world's international traffic command. Stop. Surprised, she did, mid-word in mid-sentence.

He waited until her agitated breathing had subsided and a faint sense of embarrassment swept over her. Then he spoke very quietly.

"Before I tell you what forgiveness is, I am going to tell you about our Superior, Brother Swithin."

IX

"When he was fifteen, walking home from school one late afternoon in November - it was already dark - he was attacked from behind by a man who dragged him into a deserted garage and sodomized him."

At her involuntary gasp he paused merely to say tonelessly, "Oh yes, you needn't think rape is the sole prerogative of women," before continuing.

"Brother Swithin - not his name then, of course - fought back as best he could, but he was never a strong lad, always small for his age apparently, and his attacker had a knife. Nevertheless I gather he made things pretty difficult before he finally gave in. Which may have been why the attacker - after he had finished - decided to use the knife after all, although he'd said he wouldn't. He hacked off both the boy's arms, right above the elbows. Perhaps sliced is a better word than hacked, since he was using a machete."

"Oh, God!" A year younger than her son, Julian. "And he survived?"

"He did. He staggered into the street where the local newsagent saw him."

"And did they catch him - the man?"

"That's not the point, although no, I gather they never did. The point is, the boy survived. And the boy grew into a man. And the man forgave."

"How could he?"

"Not, as you say, by forgetting. He can't forget when

he is reminded every time he uses the mechanical claws he's been given for hands. And not, as you say, by saying it doesn't matter. Of course it does, every time a stranger looks away, every time he can't do the things the rest of us can, even though he has become very accomplished with his - instruments. And certainly not by turning the other cheek."

(Was the sardonic curl of the lip intentional, a bitter acknowledgment of a sickening double entendre?)

"Perhaps if he had turned the other cheek at the time instead of resisting - but even then Brother Swithin would have seen that as acquiescing in evil, although he wouldn't have used such fancy words at that time. He only knew he mustn't give in to something so terrible and so wrong. He stopped fighting back only when the knife was at his throat and the choice was life or death. But turning the other cheek was not an option then and not feasible now, when the doer of evil is no longer present.

The evil is not an ongoing thing, as you term it, in the sense that the act of evil is finished and only the consequences remain. Consequences do not have to perpetuate evil, they can be transmuted - by spiritual alchemy. Our Lord did that." He smiled at her.

"Turning the other cheek has nothing to do with forgiving," he continued, "although it might have something to do with not seeking revenge, which might in turn be a signpost on the way. No, Brother Swithin would be the first to agree with you that forgiveness is none of these things."

"Then what is it?" She waited, afraid to breathe.

"Shall I tell you what forgiveness is?"

She nodded. Had she stumbled across the oracle at last?

"It is seeing the person - the unforgiven - as God intended him to be."

* * * * *

Marinda heard no sudden fanfare, saw no blinding flash of light. But just possibly there might have been an imperceptible lightening of the darkness and just perhaps in the far-off distance there could have been the muted sound of a single trumpet. It was definitely the best answer she had had so far.

"Thank you. I will think on this," she told him.

"Right." He spoke curtly, standing up. "You need to sign up for one of our Retreats, the sooner the better."

Marinda stared at him blankly.

"Didn't Sam tell you we are principally a Retreat House?"

She shook her head.

"Good old Sam. Well, we are. Retreats and Quiet Days. Run in conjunction with the monastery, separately of course, but held here. Some of the nuns from the Community of the Sacred Passion are coming on Monday. They'll be here for a week. That might be a good time for you to come, too. I'm sure we could slot you in, though you'll have to clear it with Brother Thaddeus on your way out - he's our Retreat Co-ordinator."

"I couldn't possibly get away for a whole week!" Besides, she had never been on a Retreat. She wasn't even that sure what it was.

"Couldn't you?" Again the black eyebrows shot up. "I thought your - problem - was a pressing one."

"Well - not that soon, anyway."

"Talk to Brother Thaddeus. But try for it. You should come. And don't kill your husband in the meantime."

She looked to see if he was joking but he didn't seem to be. Their conversation had obviously come to an end so she stood up, too.

"Come," he said. "We will pray in the Lady Chapel before you go."

As before, he led the way, but surprisingly when they reached the stairs he continued upwards instead of downwards. More bookcases on more stairs, and surely this was not the way. She had seen the chapel and it was on the ground floor. Unless there were two chapels?

There were indeed, for suddenly at rooftop level the stairs ended with a polished landing. This they crossed to enter a tiny chapel, brilliant as the illustrations in a Book of Hours, flashing jewel-like colours in all directions, Ninian Comper surely.

The low vaulted ceiling was painted bright blue with golden stars and there was a slim gold cross in the middle of the altar. A wall niche to one side held a crystal statue of Our Lady, with a candle burning in a ruby glass before it. On the other side of the altar a white candle was burning in a glass suspended from a golden chain in front of a small high safe set in the wall. The Tabernacle. So this was where the Host was reserved. And this explained the lack of Reservation in the chapel below.

Automatically she genuflected, as did Brother David.

The wooden floor, rubbed tirelessly with love and beeswax over the years, gleamed bright as glass, but she noticed it held no chairs, no benches and no pews. What on earth did the monks do during their devotions - levitate?

As if in reply, Brother David walked further into the room and knelt. Remembering he had said, "We (a definite plural) will go into the Lady Chapel to pray," she followed and knelt beside him.

"We'll begin with an Our Father," he said, and together they murmured the Lord's Prayer. She had expected to feel self conscious but the monk was going so fast she could concentrate only on keeping up with him.

Then he stood up beside her, placing both his hands on her head.

"Bless, O Lord, this thy child, granting her strength and grace and courage ..."

Marinda thought in panic of all the hairspray she had used that morning to keep her fine dark flyaway hair in place. His hands would probably stick when he tried to remove them. And her hair would be pulled up on end. She had an insane desire to laugh, which she instantly suppressed with guilt. How could she think such irrelevant, irreverent thoughts when it was really so good of him to pray for her this way, to ask such good and healing things, to care enough to pray at all? A strange contentment was settling over her; she was glad to be here in this place; it was right and good.

He was speaking so quietly now she could barely hear him, but that was all right, too, for she supposed that

God could. In fact, she realized in surprise, he was no longer even speaking in English; he seemed to have lapsed into Latin. That was probably second nature for a monk. The uniqueness of the situation was both awesome and pleasing; his hands on her head were warm and the warmth was spreading downwards through her whole body in a glow of well-being.

And still he prayed, quietly, almost inaudibly, until she began to realize it wasn't Latin she was hearing at all, nor in fact any language she knew, nor even recognizable words. She knew then what it had to be. He was speaking in tongues.

Strange little trills and soft vocal sounds repeated themselves, filling her ears, flooding her being with warmth. It was like a cloak enfolding her now, this unmistakeable, spreading warmth, bringing not just comfort and well-being but a wonderful rising almost tangible sense of joy.

When he stopped at last she did not, could not speak, knew it was not even necessary to speak, as she genuflected again and followed him in silence back down the stairs.

* * * * *

He left her in the wide part of the hall just before it opened into the conservatory; she could see the white chairs and geraniums through the arch, and beyond them the door to the other chapel. Here, where they were standing, there was a desk, and on the wall beside it a bulletin board and a large clock ticking. It seemed to be a rudimentary, almost temporary, kind of office. No one was at the desk.

"Brother Thaddeus will come," said Brother David, striking the gong on the desk with the small wooden mallet lying beside it. "You can sort out Retreat dates with him. But sooner rather than later."

"Yes," she nodded, sensing his desire to go. "And - thank you." Inadequate, but what words wouldn't be?

He smiled, briefly and beautifully, and withdrew.

She stood listening to the loud ticking of the clock, hoping Brother Thaddeus would not be long. Five minutes passed. She was finding it difficult to stand still and there was no chair to sit on, unless she took the one behind the desk which she didn't feel would be appropriate. She was still in a daze of euphoria, longing to be outside in the sun, wanting to sing in the privacy of her car, to twirl and laugh somewhere alone in her house. The warmth from Brother David's prayers still covered her like a magic cloak and she wondered if it would always be so, whether she would ever need to wear a coat or a cardigan again.

The clock ticked on. But beyond that she could hear, or thought she could hear, something else, the smallest of sounds — a faint occasional clicking - from an open door behind the desk. Perhaps it was Brother Thaddeus working. Perhaps he had not heard the gong.

Hesitantly she walked around behind the desk to peer through the open doorway but the small room beyond was empty. It was more of a legitimate office, however; she could see a telephone and an electric typewriter on that desk. There seemed to be an even further room beyond that, whose door was also ajar (the whole place must be a rabbit warren of rooms) and it was from there the small sound was coming. Like the point of a ball-point pen being flicked in and out. Repeatedly.

Surely it could do no harm to knock on this second door and ask for Brother Thaddeus? It would be far more unobtrusive than sounding the gong again herself; she would not have dared that, and by now she was firmly convinced the other gong had not been heard.

So, crossing this second space, she tapped lightly on the door frame, looking inside just in time to see a man give a startled jump and drop a small box onto a table. Paper clips and rubber bands spilled out everywhere.

"I'm so sorry!" she blurted, "I didn't mean - I shouldn't have - I was just looking for -"

The monk - for of course it was a monk - turned around to look at her. He was small, fortyish and bald as an egg.

"It's all right," he said gently, reaching for the upturned box and scattered bits.

"Let me help, please," she said, starting forward, then stopping suddenly as she saw the long metal claws he was using in place of hands.

"It's all right," he repeated, looking at her from behind hexagonal rimless glasses. And his eyes were the kindest she had ever seen.

She did not know now whether to help or not and glanced quickly around the small room full of filing cabinets. One drawer stood open. A folder lay on the floor with papers spilling out of it, and thinking he must have dropped that, too, she bent to retrieve it.

"Behold," he said, expertly picking out and holding up a single elastic circle with one of his split claws, "the humble rubber band. One of man's greatest inventions. God creates, and in His image man, too, creates. The breath of life I owe to God. The continuing breath I owe to rubber bands." He laughed merrily, ending with a truly gay and beatific smile.

She knew instantly and intuitively what he meant. The staggering, bleeding boy, the shocked newsagent who would have had no time, material nor expertise for tourniquets. But he would have had rubber bands. Rubber bands for newspapers. Rubber bands for tourniquets. Thick, tight, plentiful, right there on his counter. He would have slipped them over the stumps of the bleeding arms. And they would have worked.

Yes, praise be for rubber bands she thought, as he deftly continued to pick them up, his mechanical elbows bending and straightening, clicking as they locked into place, with the soft metallic sounds she had heard earlier.

Then muted running footfalls sounded behind them, as a flushed and panting Brother Thaddeus appeared.

"Oh Father Swithin, forgive me, I'm so sorry, I didn't know you were here, I'm so sorry, Mrs. Lawson, I should have come the minute the gong sounded..."

And I should have stayed beside it, she thought grimly, while aloud she said, "No, it's my fault." Which of course it was.

She followed him meekly back to the first desk, thinking the hallway was like a river running through the building, and the part now where they were standing, where it widened to hold the empty desk and the calendar on the wall, was the delta of the river ...

"I met Brother David on the stairs. He says to put you down for a Retreat. Do you work? Can you come next week?" He had pulled out a pencil from the desk drawer; she could see a number of detailed markings on the calendar, too far away to read.

"I don't have a job, if that's what you mean, but I'll have to arrange things for my youngest and for the household, and that may take a little time." It was all so fast, like wading into the current of an unknown river; she needed more time. "I think next week is too soon."

"Well -" Brother Thaddeus looked doubtful. "There's an independent group coming Tuesday week, just for four days, business types from the city, - ah, but the next lot," he brightened with enthusiasm as he continued speaking, "from a parish in Pimlico, are a really super lot. They come every year. What about coming when they do?"

"How long for?"

"A week."

"I really couldn't. Let's go back to the businessmen." She was apprehensive but four days sounded manageable. "Would they mind? Does it really matter if I don't work in the City and if I'm female?"

"Oh no - there'll be ladies among them, at least one solicitor and a banker. And nobody minds. After all, apart from the initial coffee and introductory talk, the whole thing is done in silence. That's the whole point."

"Then it doesn't matter who else comes when I do."

"Well, it sort of does."

Brother Thaddeus was so earnest, so anxious to

explain, that her heart went out to him and again she was reminded of her son Octavian.

"For one thing," he continued, "we can't have more than fifteen at a time because we only have fifteen guest rooms. And the talks are geared to who's here. For instance, the CSP Sisters will get a different emphasis than the City folk, because as Religious, they already understand the basics -" the blue eyes faltered for a moment in embarrassment at his possibly patronizing words.

"That's more than I do," she confided with a sudden smile, thinking that of all the Brothers she had yet seen, the son-like Thaddeus was by far the most approachable. "I've never been on a Retreat and I don't really know what it's all about."

"Don't worry," he said, twisting the pencil in long, sensitive fingers. "It's just time alone with God. Organized time, with hours for prayer, or meditation, interspersed with talks - little homilies or mini-sermons - from one of us. There's daily Mass of course, and the rest of the services. People - you lot - are silent the whole time, which actually takes a lot of pressure off when you realize you don't have to worry or think about what you're going to say. You're supposed to be retreating from the world, and catching a glimpse of another way of life - ours. Don't worry, it's easy. Quiet and peaceful and you often get surprising results. Brother David seemed pretty definite that you should come."

She nodded. She might as well give it a try. What could she lose?

"Then I'll put you down for the four-day one Tuesday week."

"The City folk?"

He nodded. You're lucky. Father Swithin is Retreat Conductor for that one. He'll be giving the talks."

"Okay." Then almost as an afterthought, "How much does it cost?"

"We ask for a donation of ten pounds a day if you can afford it. That's everything, room and board and no VAT."

She nodded, amazed that it could cost so little. As he was writing her name on the calendar she spoke again.

"Do you mind if I ask you something? I thought, as monks, you were all called Brother. But you said Father Swithin just now."

"Oh, right. We are all Brothers but most of us are ordained priests as well, so technically we're Fathers, too. That's why the locals call us, "The Godfathers". He grinned. "But Brother Swithin is our Father Superior and so we usually call him Father. Not always."

She nodded and was about to speak again when a melodious little bell somewhere in the far depths of the building sounded three times. Brother Thaddeus straightened and closed his eyes, his lips moving silently. Again the bell rang three times, and then again, and then there was a multiplication of nine rings.

His eyes snapped open and he smiled, as he explained, "The Angelus. We say it wherever we are, but I know I'd forget if it weren't for the bell." He looked at the wall where the clock said twelve. "Are you staying for sex?"

He continued speaking through Marinda's unguarded look of astonishment, with only the sudden wave of colour passing across his face to indicate that he had

117

understood her misunderstanding. "It's at 12:45," he continued, "in the main chapel. You are welcome to wait there if you'd like to stay."

"No, I have to be getting back," she mumbled, thinking how truly base she was to have allowed her ears to mishear the final "t" of that service. It had been clearly printed outside the chapel. Sext.

But she laughed in the car as she drove away. Relief and hysteria, humour, gratitude, joy. But most of all and over it all the magic warmth from the unknown prayers of Brother David. She had been in the monastery for two hours and knew that in that time both her life and outlook had been altered and changed forever in some indefinable way. She had glimpsed the eternal perspective. Forgiveness. Brother Swithin. If he had managed it, then anyone could. But how? By seeing the man as God intended him to be. But how?

"Please, God," she murmured aloud in the car - and it did not seem silly to be doing so - "make Michael as he used to be."

Was it wrong to want the past returned? Uneasily she shifted her weight, intuition kicking in with the truth even while her mind revolved and circled, crammed with thoughts enough for a lifetime.

She drove back through the autumn world of Richmond Park, an enchanted world where all the trees and even the grass had been dusted with gold. A fantasy world which seemed to be caught and held unmoving in a crystal ball of silence. She imagined a giant's hand reaching out to pick it up and hold it like a child's toy, this crystal ball of a world, hold it and shake it and turn it upside down, so that it would move again and be filled not with whirling flakes of snow but with swirling flecks of gold. A giant's hand. Only the hand of God could turn the world upside down. And make Michael as he used to be.

X

"The Godfathers? Sounds like a pub! Let's face it, darling, you came out of that place on a high and it'll wear off like any other high. Then you'll feel worse than ever, just like with any other hangover. Honestly, people deal with religion at their peril!"

Thus spake Susan Fisher, Judy's mother, Jeremy's mother, ex-actress and ex-wife. For no sooner had Marinda re-entered her house than the phone had started ringing. Thus did the world shatter the crystal silence she had carried so carefully from the monastery.

Suddenly it was as if she could see a large motorway sign in her mind, the kind with illuminated moving letters, on which her intuition was spelling out a message. T-h-i-s - i-s - w-h-y, the letters flashed, R-e-t-r-e-a-t-s - a-r-e - n-e-c-e-s-s-a-r-y, - s-o - t-h-a-t - a - t-h-o-u-g-h-t - c-a-n - b-e - t-h-o-u-g-h-t - a-n-d - f-e-l-t - a-n-d - h-e-l-d - e-v-e-n - t-o - c-o-n-c-l-u-s-i-o-n, - w-i-t-h-o-u-t - i-n-t-e-r-r-u-p-t-i-o-n. Yes, and without telephones.

"Darling! Where have you been? I've been trying to ring for ages. You're never there. Rosa said she didn't know where you'd gone."

"Not far and I'm back now." Marinda liked Susan and always warmed to 'darling' even though she knew Susan, with her theatrical background the most 'luvvy' of 'luvvies', used it indiscriminately. Susan and Michael had met years ago in 'rep', and for many years the four of them had maintained a close friendship, right up until the time Susan's husband had deserted, in fact. Although she had to admit Michael's drinking was beginning to put a strain on the relationship even before that. "So how are you, Susy?"

"Darling, how are you?" Then lowering her voice she added, "Is Michael there?"

"Not at the moment."

"Well, I know something's wrong. Tell me about it!"

"Why do you say that?"

"I could tell when you dropped Judy off after school yesterday. You looked - well, really stressed out. Couldn't say anything in front of the girls, of course, and didn't dare call afterwards - figured Michael would be around. So now - come on, out with it!"

"Well, it's just more of the usual."

"Michael drinking?"

"Mmm."

"I'm so glad I'm out of all that, darling, and that King Rat is no longer in the picture. I wouldn't live with a man again if you paid me. Not that I don't like them. I do, as a species - you know, their nice low voices and hairy arms. But I wouldn't want one as a pet around the house again."

"What about Jeremy?"

"A son is a different thing. Which reminds me, I had a postcard yesterday. They were in Sedona, Arizona. A picture of real John Wayne territory - all those big red rocks."

"I think I told you the last card Septimus sent was when they were in New Orleans. They do seem to be enjoying it."

"Of course they are. They'll remember it the rest of their lives. But back to the subject, darling. Michael's misbehaviour."

"I don't like to - I feel guilty when I talk about it."

"Why?"

"Disloyal."

"Not if it helps. Look, darling, women have to stick together. That's why we have lots of close friends and men haven't. Over the centuries we've been the downtrodden slave half of the human race. And do you know what's made it bearable? Only our camaraderie - even if it's unseen and unspoken camaraderie."

"You mean camaraderie like Linda Carson's?" It was an unfair blow; Linda Carson was the woman Susan's King Rat husband had run off with, but somehow Susan always left Marinda feeling inexplicably defensive on behalf of men. They were under attack these days, beleaguered, and it really wasn't fair. Deep down in spite of her protests, she felt that Susan was a man-hater.

"There are exceptions, of course." An edge of ice had inserted itself into Susan's voice, though it melted almost as quickly as it had formed. "But come on, darling - speak."

Marinda did speak. Over the past months she had confided massively in her friend, but the confidences were censored. Susan knew about Michael's drinking and most of the quarrels; she did not know about his incontinence nor the occasional DT's, when he was convinced their bed was crawling with ants. She knew Michael no longer ate with his family and that this caused Marinda great distress, and she both knew and guessed that Marinda was very near a breaking point. She did not know the great fear which haunted her now, a fear that she might actually murder Michael, the fear which had driven her, however indirectly, to the Godfathers.

It had been a relief to talk to Susan about these things and she talked again now of her visit to the monastery, of the Brothers she had met. She spoke of Brother David, his wisdom and his humour, but she did not speak of the actual moment when he had placed his hands upon her head and spoken in tongues. That was a secret, sacred thing, the warmth of which still held her in a kind of after-glow. But she spoke of the Retreat now booked, and of her hope, and of how magic and golden the drive home had been.

"A high, darling, you're on a high, that's all. Well, you're an artist, so of course you're going to see things in terms of space and colour. But it's all so superficial. You should try theosophy, like me," she continued, "for real peace of mind."

"I don't think so," Marinda said. "I don't believe in recycled human beings."

"You might not be a recycled human being. Or you might not become one. You might be reincarnated as a bird. Or a deer."

"No, thanks." But she did then tell her friend about the deer she had hit two days ago in Richmond park. "I was thinking about Henry VIII at the time, you know, and how awful he was and how he sort of looks like Michael looks now - his mouth, anyway -and how he hunted deer, and then I sort of aimed the car at them both."

"Michael and the deer?"

"Michael and Henry VIII. I didn't mean to hit the poor deer at all."

"Your problem, darling," drawled Susan in her smoker's contralto, "is that you have too much imagination. Which again comes from being an artist. But you should have rung me up about the deer in the first place, darling. It doesn't help to keep things like that to yourself."

"Probably not."

"At least I was right to feel things weren't going well for you. After all, they didn't cast me as Madam Arcati in Blithe Spirit for nothing. It was type-casting; I have a feel for these things and it shows." (Blithe Spirit had been her most successful stage play and it still found its way into most of her conversations.) "If I hadn't known that myself I might have guessed it from Heather's behaviour."

"Heather?" It was unusual for anyone to complain of Heather. "Why? You mean when she stayed overnight for Judy's birthday? What did she do?"

"She didn't do anything. She just seemed very quiet and withdrawn, not like her old self at all."

"Oh, dear."

Picking up the concern in that mild exclamation, Susan spoke more gently. "It's bound to affect the kids, darling. You really should boot him out."

"Could you have booted King Rat out?"

There was a bitter sigh at the other end of the line. "Touché. Wish I had. I hung on too long, thinking where there's life, there's hope. K.R. must have been amused."

"Oh, I don't know. I think K.R. must be envious of you

now. Your TV commercials are a runaway success. He must see them all the time." Marinda's arm was getting tired from holding the phone. Telephone chats with Susan could last an hour or more.

"Commercials pay the bills, which probably eases his conscience. But it's not the same as real acting, you and I both know that. I'm prostituting my art."

"No, you're not, Susy. I'd give anything if Michael could get a commercial."

"What? Are you actually pointing a kind thought in that man's direction? Has your trip to the Godfathers produced a miracle after all?"

"I don't mean for the money," Marinda hurried on, embarrassed, "but just so he could feel - well, back in the world again, his world. Your world. I think it would make all the difference. After all, your face is seen and known; a director might easily think of you for a part. And when your agent proposes you, they know who he's talking about. And it must be fun being recognized in Sainsbury's."

"Oh, I suppose so." There was a reluctant purring in her tone.

"But listen, Susy - I really have to go. Octavian is moving back in today - did I tell you?"

"You told me he was coming but you didn't say when. That's nice."

"He's just started at RADA."

"I know. Even nicer."

"And nice that Michael's away while he moves in. There's more than a little friction there."

"I'm not surprised. Two bulls in the same paddock. You can't really go against nature, darling."

"We'll see. Anyway, we'll be in touch."

"We will indeed. Take care, darling. Bye."

"Bye."

She replaced the receiver, thinking how quickly and totally she had plunged back into the real world. It had only taken one phone call and already she had to close her eyes to remember the voice of Brother David. And yet wasn't there still - yes, there was - an infinitesimal inner peace, a residue of his strange blessing.

* * * * *

How mature Octavian was. The rush of pleasure as he stepped through the door was also a shock of surprise, for self-assured, tall and handsome as a cliché, he had crossed the final line between boyhood and manhood since she had last seen him. How had this happened? Had it been that long? They spoke frequently on the telephone, but she tried now to remember the last sighting, surely only weeks - could it have been months? - ago.

It was time, of course it was time at twenty-two when he had already finished university and a year of law school. The possibilities of manhood, always recognized as eventual certainties, had long been there in abundance, the height, the shaving, the deepened voice. But suddenly they had come together, jelled into completion, so that it was not a youth now but a man who stood in the doorway kissing his mother and hugging his little sister. And yes, she was surprised but it was surprise already beginning to be modified and tinged with memory. Had she not had the same reaction the last time she had seen him, sometime during the summer?

He had been a man then, too, and she had been astonished – yet when he had gone, her thoughts had reverted, turned back to hold him again as a youth in her mind, a boy. Was this trick of memory an attempt to stave off her own mortality or merely part of her current desire to revive the past, to resurrect the man who had fathered this first-born son?

How handsome this tall son now was with his fair hair and ice-blue eyes. Brother Thaddeus did not have the same colouring and he was not handsome nor nearly so tall. There was really no similarity at all between them and she wondered why she had ever thought there was. Or why she was thinking of him now. She should be thinking of Michael, whose resemblance to his son was slight but recognizable, definitely recognizable.

"Where's Dad?"

"Doing a bit of filming in Ireland." It was an unprepared lie, the first thing that came into her head and she was instantly ashamed of it. Yet she couldn't tell him the truth now in front of Heather, that Michael had gone off in a huff without an explanation or any indication of when he would return.

"Does he know I'm coming?"

"I told him you wanted to. We didn't get around to discussing it in detail."

"Oh, Mum -" The lost child was back for an instant in the fleeting uncertainty now crossing his face. "I should have spoken to him myself. Or written."

"Nonsense! This is your home and always will be. And

no child of mine will ever have to ask permission to come home!"

He gave her another hug and laughed an uncertain laugh. "Good old Mum."

Heather, repeatedly tugging his blazer during all this, now tugged even harder. "Octopus," she said, using the old family nick-name they used to tease him with, "would you like to see my bird drawings for school?"

"Bird droppings?" He was not above teasing back.

"Nooo!" she squealed in mock frustration. "Drawings! And would you like to play some scrabble?"

"Love to, honeypot," he answered, ruffling her hair, picking up one of his bags, "as soon as I get unpacked. Same room, Mum?"

"The same room. Rosa's been through it like an army!"

He laughed again. And for awhile they pretended, the three of them, for the whole weekend and two days afterwards, with Rosa happily fluttering around them in the mornings and the three of them eating together in the evenings or just passing each other in the hallways or other rooms, occasionally calling out to each other. And always there was laughter. She hadn't realized how much she had missed the laughter of her children. If only Septimus and Julian and Sebastian could be there, too. She did a finger calculation of half-term breaks and an airline schedule but knew it did not compute, that it would be Christmas before all her children would be under her roof again.

But right now she, Octavian and Heather were happy, as if they were sitting at a picnic in a pocket of bright sunlight, even though a rainstorm was approaching from all directions. She could see it painted on a surreal canvas, the piercing clarity of the sunlight, each blade of grass a clear unearthly, painfully beautiful green. It could not last. The blue-black storm, laced with lightning, was surrounding them. But not with them yet. Not yet. Not quite yet.

* * * * *

It broke early on Wednesday morning, first a wind as his taxi drew up, then the light pattering of rain as he reached the door, and finally the full force of the storm as he wrenched it open and entered the house. And yet, Marinda thought months later, that wasn't the worst of the storm at all although it had seemed so at the time. It was merely the forerunner of a massive hurricane gathering in the distance, slowly thickening, swirling, and beginning to move in their direction.

XI

"Hello, Dad."

"I see you're here."

"I am. But just ready to go out the door for an early class. How was the filming?"

Michael did not reply, striding past Octavian to set his suitcase down at the foot of the stairs.

"Hello, Michael." Marinda appeared at the door of the kitchen. She tried to make the greeting cheerful, although she made no movement towards her husband. Heather crouched behind her. We're all behaving like frightened rabbits, she thought in irritation, and I will not have it. There must be a way out, a way back. "Would you like some coffee?"

A car horn sounded outside and Heather sprinted for the door, looking neither to right nor left.

"Heather!" her father commanded, "Come here!"

But the child was already outside the door, running, her voice ringing back through the rain, "Mrs. Fisher's waiting!"

The anger on his face was well controlled as Marinda interceded with attempted lightness, "She hates being late for school," just as she noticed the girl's sky-blue school blazer still lying on the chair in the hall beside her satchel of books.

"So do I, grinned Octavian, "so I'm running, too. But it's great to have you back, Dad. We'll have to talk tonight."

"No," his father replied evenly, "we will talk now."

"But I'll be late."

"There are things to be settled."

An instant of anger crossed his son's face, giving way to instant resignation. This was, after all, his father. Facing him now it was difficult to remember he himself was no longer a child. The temptation still was to quake in fear. "Very well," he said reluctantly.

The reaction was not lost on his father who wanted respect above all else from his son, craved it, felt it his due. What he was getting instead was a guarded fear. All right. If he couldn't have respect he would settle for fear. He led the way into the kitchen.

"Here," he said, sitting at the antique refectory table which still held their breakfast things. "You can bring some coffee," he nodded in Marinda's direction. They were the first words he had addressed to her.

She filled three mugs - incongruously cheerful with their painted yellow sunflowers - and sat down at the table herself, even though she sensed this was not in Michael's plan.

His hand shook badly as he reached for his coffee. "So there has been a fait accompli the minute my back was turned."

"Well, Dad -" Octavian spread his hands with an attempted laugh. "Neither your back nor your front was here and I had to get out of the flat. Didn't you know I wanted to come?"

"I may have been told, but no decision had been taken," his father replied with the cold formality of a board meeting.

"Why the delay? There wasn't a committee sitting on it, was there?" There was a beginning edge of impatience in Octavian's voice. Then, "Were you going to refuse me?" he asked quietly.

"Never!" came from Marinda.

Octavian shot her a desperate look of gratitude before turning again to his father.

"Possibly not," Michael conceded stiffly. "But I cannot see why you would give up law school for RADA. It doesn't make sense."

"How can you say that, Dad, you of all people? If acting's in your blood, it's there, that's all there is to it, and it's in mine. I love it. I love the whole ambience, the stagecraft and lighting, the mouthing of other words, another's words, the movement, the theories, the slipping into another identity like you slip into another jacket, getting absolutely rid of yourself - and I got all this from you, inherited it, I must have. Can't you see? I should have faced it before, admitted it. Only you wanted me so much to be a barrister ..."

A flicker of something - pride, understanding or perhaps nostalgia for his own lost youth - stirred in Michael's face so that he hesitated before asking, "And just how long do you propose living here?" His bluster was fading in spite of all he could do.

"The course lasts three years and I started three weeks ago. Look - they've given me a scholarship for tuition; all I really need is a place to live in the meantime. And eat." He smiled disarmingly, while Marinda silently placed his favourite pork and mushroom casserole on the menu for that evening.

"Maybe -" his enthusiasm was beginning to waver now ever so slightly - "we can work out how much it will cost you; I'll keep track of it as a debt, and then start repaying you afterwards when I'm working."

"No," Marinda whispered, blinking back tears. "That's not the way it's going to be. It's simply not." She turned to Michael, blazing eyes seeking his.

But he avoided them, his own eyes puffy and hooded, emotionless as he ignored her.

"That's certainly a possibility," he said to Octavian. "But you're going to learn just how difficult the profession is. You're not going to just walk into a National Theatre production, you know, or straight into a film." The boy's smile infuriated him. Even the fear he had inspired on his arrival was now dwindling pathetically and he did not know how to retrieve it, except by sneering.

"I do know, Dad. Of course I do. But I've got to try."

In the silence that followed they all heard the scratching of a key in the front door lock. Then the door itself swung open and Rosa scuttled into the hall, to their mutual relief.

"Ah, Senor Michael!" Her face lit up with religious fervour at the sight of her saint. "And Senora. And Octavian!" Her smile broadened further as she spoke each name; her cup was indeed running over as she entered the kitchen.

They nodded and greeted her separately together, the two actors immediately reverting to normalcy so that no one, least of all Rosa, would have guessed the awkwardness of the scene she had just interrupted.

"I'll be off now," Octavian said, scraping back his chair, kissing his mother and heading for the door. "I'm running late."

"Goodbye," his father answered, also rising, unable to resist smiling for the audience of his most devoted fan, now watching him with starstruck eyes. His smile widened. His teeth were still among his best assets, large, even and uncrowned.

Only Marinda sat frozen to the spot, incapable of moving as Rosa poured her own mug of coffee.

"The kitchen, shall I clear her before the drawing room, Senora?"

"No. Thank you anyway, Rosa, but I'll do it. You just carry on upstairs."

Rosa nodded, hyperventilating slightly at the sight of Michael's back retreating up the stairs with his suitcase. She sighed as she opened the cleaning cupboard, removing the duster, the polish and the hoover, somehow managing to balance them all with her mug of coffee as she started to climb the stairs herself. Then Marinda heard her stop and click her tongue, turn around, deposit the cleaning gear.

She returned to the door of the kitchen holding Heather's blazer and books, looked mournfully at Marinda and shrugged her shoulders. "Pobrecita!" she said, rolling her eyes in sympathy.

Marinda nodded. "I know, Rosa. She forgot them. I hope she won't get into too much trouble about it."

She sat a few moments longer at the table with her cold mug of coffee. It had been an upsetting morning, unforeseen and unrehearsed. She had not known

Michael was going to return at this point, nor had she anticipated the discussion that would follow when he did. That, too, had been upsetting, but it was more than simply Michael's animosity towards his son. She was worried about Octavian on some other deeper level.

What was it he had said? That he wanted to slip on another identity, get out of himself. No, not out, get rid of himself. To be sure, he was speaking of acting, but she recognized a cry far deeper than that, far more than that. He was home - yes, for a practical reason, but also in effect he was stepping back into the nest of childhood. He had changed direction absolutely. Did he not want to grow up? Did he not want to be the self he saw in the mirror, this beautiful son? What was it? Or was it simply her own dissolving brain? The days had long passed when she could have spoken to his father about him.

She thought of the young slim hands of Brother Thaddeus with the nails bitten deep into the quick. He was as sensitive, as full of compassion as Octavian. He had truly cared about the deer she had killed in the park. Octavian would also have cared had he known about it, would have cared deeply. And his nails, too, were deeply bitten.

* * * * *

The phone rang with Susy's minor miracle, or so it seemed at the time.

"Darling - I don't suppose Michael's back yet?"

"Just this morning. Let's talk another time."

"No, no, darling, he's the one I want - but wait - not for a minute. You'll never guess what I've managed!" Her voice was triumphant, her words careering up and down the tonal scale, bumping into each other with excitement.

"Well, why don't you tell me?"

"You know my new tea commercial? Of course you don't because I haven't done it yet. Anyway, darling, it's going to be a whole series of one-minute commercials built around what kind of tea I give everybody - I'm this Superwoman Executive - and everybody from the vicar to the plumber to the banker and the builder and my lover and solicitor, they all get a cup of tea from me - you can see the possibilities are endless!"

"I can indeed."

"Well, I've got the only speaking role but they need a man for all the other roles and they think it would be a clever gimmick to use the same one in a different costume each time. I told them I'd like to have Michael Lawson and they agreed to consider him."

"Oh, Susy!"

"Of course he won't make as much as I do and he might think the whole thing is beneath him -"

"That's not the point. He'd be working!"

"I remember you saying that the last time we spoke, when I was complaining about it and you said how you wished he could do a commercial - and darling, we can play it down, make it seem he's more or less doing me a favour."

"I think it's a splendid idea! Susy, you really are a true friend."

"Tut, tut, my dear," came the pleased, throaty theatrical reply, "it's nothing."

But it was a great deal. Beneath Susan Fisher's brash exterior, the wisecracks and the too-blond hair, there dwelt a strangely conservative creature, sensitive, caring and kind. And Marinda had always known that the wittily caustic remarks about the erring King Rat were no more than camouflage to cover a broken heart.

"The thing is, darling," Susy was continuing, "they'd like to see him. He hasn't actually been in anything for a long time, you know. So I suggested - ooh, I can't believe they're really going to do this - I suggested they pop round here for a drink and I'd see if I could get you two over."

"They're coming to you? Susy, that just doesn't happen." She could still remember Michael attending formal try-outs in a hall, an unused theatre, sometimes even a hotel room, even when the part had already been offered to him through his agent. It was part of the ritual, the protocol of casting. A director would simply never come to the actor's house for a try-out.

"It's just Rupert and Nick, darling, and they're doing it as a special favour to me. I always get them when the commercial comes through Ramsay and Ramsay."

"Who are Rupert and Nick - director and producer?"

The unseen Susy shook her head. "Director and writer. You'll like them. And they like me. In fact, Rupert has more than a director's eye on me, I think - so I thought I'd put it to the test."

"I hope you're not parting with that jewel more precious than life itself just for Michael's career?"

A throaty laugh of delight came through the receiver. "Pawning it, maybe. Anything to help a friend. We'll see.

Anyway, drinks chez moi - okay?"

"When?" Marinda was poised for panic at the sound of the word drink.

"This evening."

"Good heavens! I don't know - look Susy, you'll have to be the one to ask Michael. If I did it, I know he'd turn it down flat. Ring him and ask him. My guess is he'll be over the moon about it. And tonight's fine as far as I'm concerned. But if he okays it, can we come fairly early?"

"The drinking?"

"Yes. Obviously it's worse as the evening wears on."

"I hope I'm not sticking my neck out."

"I hope so, too."

"Who's his agent?"

"Michael Myers."

"Then leave it to me. Of course he still might have to show up for a try out later on, but this ought to clinch it."

"Look, I'm going to hang up now so you can ring him. I'm not going to say a word about it myself. I know nothing about it, okay?"

"Okay, darling."

"And, Susy?"

"Yes?"

"Thanks more than I can say."

Putting the phone down she recognized another problem, minor but it mattered. Michael wouldn't pick up the phone if anyone else was in the house. "It won't be for me," he had once said when she had run in from the garden to answer the persistent ringing, only to see him sitting an arm's length from the telephone in the study. "It won't be for me," he had repeated in petulant answer to her query.

Now when Susy rang back the same thing would be apt to happen, he would let it go on ringing forever, assuming either she or Rosa would pick it up. She must not arouse suspicion by doing so, for if he even remotely suspected this was a plan she and Susy had concocted (and worse, a charitable plan), the whole thing would fall through. Whereas now there was the tiniest ray of hope.

What a fool I am, she thought, not to give up. But on the other hand, who knows, who knows what may come of this?

She told Rosa she was going out briefly. She told her not to answer the phone if it rang. Rosa merely nodded, curiosity not being one of her attributes. Whatever instructions should be given by her icon's wife, this comforting and comely Senora with whom she felt such simpatica, they would be fine with Rosa.

Marinda grabbed her keys from the kitchen, calling out as she walked to the door, "I'm just off to the post office and to do a few errands." There was no reply but she knew he had heard her.

All this subterfuge for the sake of a phone call. She hated lying but lying was all right if the intention was right. Or was it? That meant the end justified the means, and that was swampy territory indeed for one who always sought the terra firma of moral absolutes. She didn't want to deceive, knowing deception was born of fear. Nor did she want to live like this, she thought, closing the door. In fear and deception.

* * * * *

But it worked. Michael met her on her return, stepping out of the study as soon as she opened the front door, almost as if he had been waiting for her. Which he had.

"Susan Fisher rang," he said, carefully casual, not meeting her eyes. "Apparently they want me for one of her commercials."

"Oh? That might be fun." She, too, was careful to sound casual, not overly enthusiastic.

"I said I'd think about it."

"Are you supposed to phone back?" She would continue the charade for however long it took.

"She's having the writer and director over for a drink this evening and asked if we'd like to come. I could see if I liked them."

"Good idea."

"I'm off for the Garrick now."

Noticing the smoked-salmon-and-cucumber striped tie, she blurted out, "But it's only Wednesday!", knowing Thursday was his usual day for the club, knowing too that he might drink even more there than he would at home in the middle of the day, depending on who he ran into. He mustn't be drunk before the evening even started. Afterwards she could have kicked herself for protesting, knowing it would be a relief just to have him safely out of the house. Safely. Yes, that was the word. Her old fear still gnawed at the edge of awareness.

"I thought I'd see what I can find out about them. Obviously they're small fry or I would have heard of them."

"Why not ask Michael Myers?"

"I don't want to bother my agent yet. Better size them up myself first. I might not want anything to do with them." He made no reference to the fact that it was they who had not contacted his agent first in the usual manner.

But there was no disguising the underlying excitement in his bearing, the new sense of self-worth behind the arrogant words, the sense of hope. And he had wanted to share it with her.

As he passed the hall mirror on the way out he drew himself up taller by another inch, nodding proudly, half jestingly, to his own reflection in a way that reminded her ... reminded her ... and wrung her heart.

XII

They walked to the Fisher house at Marinda's suggestion. "It's only fifteen minutes," were the words she used; the words she did not use being: 'You won't be fit to drive later and it will save an argument if I try to take my car.'

Octavian had returned in time to babysit his delighted sister. "I'll make spaghetti bolognese," he winked, while she clapped her hands.

It was a pretty walk down a long street of little Victorian houses with brightly flowering window boxes and stained glass doors, then past the small shops of Barnes village itself, onto the Terrace beside the Thames where the houses were still small but much older.

Susan Fisher's house was listed, a little gem from the eighteenth century whose brass door knocker was in the shape of a fish. The first drops of rain were just beginning to fall as Michael hammered the knocker against its stud. It was a major mistake not to have brought umbrellas.

"Darlings!" their hostess cried as she opened the door in flowing orange silk trousers and tunic, "You've made it just in time - the heavens are going to open! Come in, come in to the three of us!"

Marinda was astonished to find them so young. Not Susan, of course, in her early forties like Marinda herself, but the two men with her. Rupert Isaacs, short with thinning hair, still couldn't have been more than thirty-one or two, while Nicholas McIntyre, tall and gawky, could only be in his twenties, early twenties at that. She could sense that Michael was equally taken aback; from the corner of her eye she recognized the familiar faint animosity in the stiffness of his posture as he tried hard not to pant after the rapid walking. How old he must seem to them at fifty-two in his slacks, his carefully tied cravat and silk shirt, these young men in their tight designer jeans and jackets.

And he looked even older, she thought anxiously, so much older because of the puffiness around his eyes and the bluish tinge to his cheeks and nose. Prussian blue with a touch of titanium white - was it only her artist's eye assigning colour? But perhaps it was going to be a black and white commercial, you never knew these days.

If only his face were on canvas, how quickly she could repair it! Two light brush strokes and the cheekbones would reappear, one quick shading along the cheeks and temples and the lean, craggy, appealing face would re-emerge. It was all still there, underneath. Surely they could see? And they would know what make-up and clever camera angles could do.

"Champagne, darlings? You have no choice; it's that or water!"

Clever of her to serve champagne, Marinda thought, not only because it lent an air of festivity (and implicit success) to the occasion but also because she would have known that Michael, like most professional drinkers, was not that keen on champagne, and so might drink less. At least as long as the champagne lasted. It would be a different story after they returned home when the drinking would continue in earnest. But who knew what might happen if he began to work again, even in a minor way, even in a commercial? With self-respect restored, in the mainstream again ...the far-off shadow of the Michael of memory beckoned distant in the sun.

"The thing we're doing is a bit like a mini-soap," Rupert ("Call me Roo") Isaacs was saying, chewing cashews with his mouth open in between gulps of champagne. "One minute sound bites out of what's obviously a dramatic situation - you know, the builder as his brick wall falls down, the barrister who's just lost his client's case, that sort of thing." He was giving Michael his full attention now, leaning forward, and Michael was listening in concentration, eyes narrowed.

"You don't have to say anything, that's for Susan here who offers a cup of tea to all these blokes. All you do is dress up and act like them. We figure it's a great comic opportunity, viewers will laugh, start waiting for the next commercial, talk about it maybe. Susan says you've had acting experience. Ever done a character role before?"

The insult hit with deadly accuracy mostly because it was unintentional. They simply had no idea who Michael was, had never seen him before. Marinda could feel the pain like a blow to her face, knowing even so that it was second-hand pain. She did not dare look at Michael, though from the corner of her eye she was aware that he had not flinched. And that is bravery, she thought, the true courage of a real trouper, a real actor, the genuine thing, too good for any of this. They should have been in the audience of Camelot, they should have seen and heard the standing ovation, they would have known then he was too good for this kind of thing.

She clenched her fists, surprised and dismayed by her own mindless surge of loyalty. She had to remind herself that he had lost all that, thrown it away. It was as well

144

they had not seen Camelot. He needed this commercial and needed it desperately. Oh please give him a chance, she willed. Please.

It was Susan who came to the rescue quickly, easily, without pause. Another trouper, Marinda thought. Actors were a wonderful lot as a species if you thought about it. Sticking together. Brotherhood in crisis. As long as they weren't competing for the same role.

"Oh Roo, darling, of course he has," she said lightly. "You'd know that if you had more to do with real theatre instead of TV. You should have seen him in Hamlet. For that matter, you should have seen me in Blithe Spirit." She licked her finger and outlined an eyebrow which produced the desired effect of laughter.

"Yes, well -" Roo looked momentarily sheepish before glancing at her admiringly. "We're always hearing about Blithe Spirit," he teased, but she had already turned to Nicholas.

"And of course you, Nick darling, couldn't really be expected to know the workings of the acting world."

"Why not? Which one of you is the producer?" Marinda asked, wanting to say something, anything.

"Oh, neither one of us, Mrs. Lawson," Nicholas answered. "I'm the writer. I work in the Commercials Dept for Ramsay and Ramsay, you see, and they've given me the Tipton's Tea account. Roo's the director who brings it all to life. But we work in tandem, you might say. I like to be in on the casting and I like to watch the filming. Sometimes I even make constructive suggestions. So does Roo - he tries to persuade me to change the wording from time to time. Sometimes he succeeds."

"Well, I do know what works and what doesn't," Roo said defensively, "just like I know who's the best cameraman and the best lighting man. By the way, this is delicious, Susy," he said, scraping the last of the onion dip out of its bowl with a soggy crisp, his eyes appreciatively on her cleavage. The warmth between them was palpable.

Marinda passed him another bowl of cashew nuts. Outside the rain was pounding in steady violence.

"More bubbly, anybody?" Susan lifted the dripping bottle from the packed ice in the silver bucket, wiping it with the white napkin she had placed beside it, refilling their glasses with the golden bubbles.

Soothed by alcohol, Michael's hands had stopped shaking. "I haven't done much TV work," he said now. "They offered me Ian of "Ian's Isle", but I was filming in Spain."

There was an awkward silence. "Must have been before my time," said Roo.

"I think I've heard of it." Nick offered. "Detective series, wasn't it?"

"No," said Michael. "A comedy series. But I never watched it. TV is really for those with nothing better to do, on whichever side of the screen."

The deliberately unpleasant remark left an even more awkward silence in the room. Marinda knew by what he had said as well as the slight thickening of his tongue that he was entering the aggressive stage of his drinking, knew he must have had a head start in the study before they had ever left home.

"Well, I'm one of those with nothing better to do,"

Susan said quickly, "and I feel damned lucky to be doing it." Whatever reservations she might feel privately, she was anxious now to save the situation.

Before anyone could reply there was a loud knocking on the door.

"Who on earth ..." Susan began with a puzzled frown just as a muffled child's voice called from upstairs, "Mummy! There's somebody at the door!"

"I know, darling!" Susan called. Marinda had forgotten Judy, obviously banished for the cocktail hour to homework or television.

"I'm certainly not expecting anybody else," Susan muttered opening the door to a tall figure standing in the deluge. "Octavian!"

"I've brought the car," he said, laughing. "Thought my parents might drown if I didn't!"

"Come in, darling," shrieked Susan, "you beautiful thoughtful creature! Give your Aunt Susan a kiss. Goodness, I haven't seen you for months and you've turned into a real man, haven't you?"

"Hello, everybody." His fair hair was blown in wet curls across his forehead, his face flushed, his navy blazer sparkling with drops of rain like sequins.

Nicholas gave an audible gasp of pleasure and astonishment while Rupert half rose from his seat. "Who," he began, "is this Greek god?"

Octavian flushed more deeply as introductions followed.

"What have you done with Heather?" Marinda asked.

"Oh, what's-her-name, the vicar's wife - Emma - came by - said you weren't expecting her but she was dropping leaflets or something. I told her you were out and I was worried because by then I'd noticed the umbrella stand was full and it's really torrential outside. We thought it would be a good idea if I brought the car over - she said she'd stay with Heather. Did I do the wrong thing?" he asked uncertainly.

"No," his mother answered dully, knowing his inclusion now was unavoidable and that his intrusion, however well intentioned, was going to be catastrophic. "It was sweet of you to be concerned and just stupid of us to leave the brollys."

"How sweet! They'd never have got a taxi, darling," Susan reassured him, "particularly when the weather's like this. Sometimes I've waited forty minutes after calling only to have them phone back and say they aren't coming because they don't have a car in the area. Have a glass of bubbly."

"I didn't mean to crash the party," Octavian said uncertainly. "I thought they might be ready to leave -"

"Nonsense!" said Nick, a reassuring hand on his shoulder. "We need you; we've just used up our own conversation. Where's the car?"

"Right outside."

"Not in the bus stop, darling?"

"No no, on the yellow line next to it," Octavian smiled, showing his perfect teeth.

"That's all right then."

There was a muffled "bup!" as Susan opened another

bottle.

"Well, just one glass," Octavian said, "After all, I'm the driver."

Michael moved his own glass aside as she approached with the bottle. "Donkey piss!" he said. "Don't you have any real drink?"

"Oh, come on, Michael, this is vintage Moet - my last bottle."

"Then I'll leave it for the rest of you." He walked to her liquor cabinet and opened it, pouring himself a half tumbler of straight scotch. "That's more like it."

Marinda's heart sank, but the Commercial duo seemed not to have noticed, their attention fully focused on Octavian.

"So you're at RADA," she heard them say, speaking as they had mentioned before, in tandem.

"We've been doing Stanislavsky," Octavian told them excitedly. I love his method, that you can think yourself into a role, actually become the character. It really seems to work."

Only Marinda heard the muffled snort from Michael's corner.

"But there's also this James Lange theory," Octavian continued, "which is fascinating. He says if you go through the motions, the emotion will follow. For instance, if you simulate fear - you know, breathe fast, widen your eyes and so on, then you'll actually start to feel fear. I don't know if that works, though we're trying it in class. But don't you think it's fascinating?"

Totally mesmerised, the duo did.

"God, isn't he wonderful?" Nick breathed to his partner, his glass and the cashews equally forgotten.

"Exactly what I had in mind," the other murmured softly. "Tipton's Tea would go right off the ratings chart."

"Good thing Equity's no longer a closed shop. They'd never have let us use him last year even if he was already at RADA."

"Let's discuss it later." Roo was sending frantic eye signals to Nick, trying to indicate Michael's presence, and finally attempting a question in Michael's direction. "Was Rada where you -"

"Gentlemen," Michael interrupted thickly, "We don't need to discuss it later. I have already made up my own mind about your little tin-pot tea commercials. I've got better things to do with my time. And now if you don't mind -" he stood up, "I'm sure you have better things to do, too. Octavian, if you're ready."

Hastily the young man stood up, setting down his half full glass. "I'm sorry," he mumbled to Nick and Roo, and another "Sorry," to Susan.

With a surprised glance at each other the two men stood as well, and in embarrassed silence watched the Lawson trio leave the house.

"I'll call you," Susan whispered to Marinda as they kissed goodbye.

Marinda only nodded, glad her tears would go unnoticed in the horizontal rain.

XIII

She arrived exhausted for the Retreat. Anxiety, fear and despair are tiring things and Marinda had spent the five days following Susan's party with all of them.

Michael himself had retreated into an alcoholic haze in the study, surrounded by boxes of old photographs which he had carried down from the studio/attic. She had thought he was moving out when she had first seen him with box after box on the stairs and her heart had contracted wildly. (Why oh why the sudden dread of his absence when his presence was even more dreadful?) But he had answered her pallor.

"You needn't worry. I haven't touched your precious paintings."

"Then what - what are -?"

"The photos," he had announced thickly, "should be sorted and catalogued. They need to be filed properly. For the record. They need to be listed. Put in albums."

As if some future historian would need them for his biography. Oh, Michael ... Her heart had contracted again, this time with an ache which had no name. "That's probably a good idea," she had said as evenly as possible.

She knew the boxed photos and snapshots concerned his minor work in the theatre, various rehearsals, shows and locations. Very few included the family - or even his major roles, which in all fairness were already in albums in the secretaire in the drawing room. As far as Marinda could tell later from the few glimpses she had when passing the study door, he was doing nothing more than looking at them. Over and over. But perhaps that was merely the initial phase. And what else was there for him to do? Turning to the past was understandable after the debacle of Susan's party - which none of them had mentioned since.

Octavian - unaware he was the cause for the new tension which had surfaced, though very much aware of its presence - had thrown himself into a frenzy of work at RADA, leaving early and returning late, his nails bitten even further down now, so far that Marinda could scarcely bear to look at their raw rims. She had noticed he was wearing band-aids on two of the worst. (This was a trivial matter, of course, one she felt she could not mention since he was no longer a child. She could only guess at the inner turmoil which manifested itself in this miniature diversion of pain.) Outwardly he was active and cheerful, teasing his little sister, singing in the shower, washing her car on the weekend, even calling out an occasional joke to his silent father in the study in a frantic parody of happiness. So that she was reminded of what might have been.

On the surface he had every reason to be happy, for on the Monday - only five days after Susan's party - he had returned from RADA brimming with excitement. He had been offered a part in a TV commercial, he told them, - a series of commercials really, for Tipton's Tea, and it was to be with Susan Fisher and it was all to do with that chance meeting with the two men at her house - wasn't it incredibly lucky? He still couldn't believe it. They had come to RADA today, the two of them, especially to speak to him about it. He'd have to do a formal try-out and they said he ought to get an agent, but one of them - Nick - seemed to think it was already in the bag. They were due to start shooting almost immediately and it wouldn't make any difference to his training at RADA, they said he should go ahead with that, that this might only be a one-off series, but just think - if it hadn't been raining that night and if he hadn't decided to take the car and pick them up, this might not have happened at all! What an amazing coincidence! What serendipity!

Knowing nothing about the real background of that night, he couldn't understand his father's silence nor his mother's half-hearted enthusiasm when he had shared his news.

"Do you think I should use your agent, Dad? Would that be okay? You know - sort of keep him in the family - what do you think?" He laughed nervously.

Michael took a long swallow of scotch before curling his thin upper lip into a sneer.

"Find your own agent."

And Octavian's smile had faded. "The thing is," he had continued, speaking rapidly now in a lower tone that was almost mumbling, "it's going to pay pretty well. So I might be able to move out again. Maybe even before Christmas," he had added uncertainly, knowing something was desperately wrong but still hoping to please them somehow. Yet he had seen his mother's eyes darken with fear at his last suggestion. What was it? What did they want him to do?

"Let's not think about that right now," Marinda had tried to sound reassuring. "Certainly not before Christmas." There didn't seem to be any way to rescue Michael nor praise her son, when either action would cancel the other.

And it was all happening too fast. She had needed to stop everything, to seize a brake, find an emergency cord, pull it, stop, get away; she gave silent fervent thanks for the forthcoming Retreat which had begun to beckon like a lifeline, a silver thread in an ink-black sea. If she could only reach it, touch it, clasp it, then just possibly it could save her, save them all. Her marriage, her family, her life seemed to be sliding into chaos; she was in control of nothing.

So she had forced herself to concentrate on the immediate, knowing she needed to organize the household for her absence even though the Retreat was only to last four days. Things needed to run smoothly and the arrangements had not been easy. For one thing, Heather was to have stayed with Judy Fisher, but that was before Susan had sprained her ankle badly and, unable to drive, had arranged for Judy herself to stay with another school friend for a week - even though Marinda had offered to postpone the Retreat so the child could stay with them.

"Don't be silly, darling, it's easier for everybody this way. You go; it might help you enormously. It can't hurt. Not the way I did with my stupid plan."

"It wasn't your fault, Susy, at least you tried."

"I do wish Heather could come, but darling, I'm really hobbling - can't even look after Judy properly."

"Don't worry. You just get better and I'll organize Heather."

"Promise me you'll go."

She had agreed. And Octavian had agreed to drive

Heather to school in the mornings for the next four days.

"Take my car," she had said, knowing they would both be unwilling to seek Michael's permission to use his BMW, permanently out of sight in the garage. That probably wouldn't even start now, Marinda reflected, since it was so seldom driven. She was often aware of this but always refrained from mentioning it for fear Michael might then decide to drive - with heaven only knew what consequences. No, it would be easier to hand Octavian her own car keys.

"As long as you don't mind dropping me at the monastery Monday evening," she told him. "Apparently we start at dawn on Tuesday morning. And if you could pick me up on Friday evening at the same time?"

"Done," Octavian agreed. "But I never thought my mother would become a nun!"

As Marinda opened her mouth to protest, he laughed. "Just kidding," for he had been highly supportive of the Retreat idea when she had announced where she was going.

Unlike Michael who had sneered and nodded, but without comment.

"And don't worry about Heather getting to school. If she doesn't mind getting there half an hour early I can still make my first class. But what about the afternoons?"

Unspoken between them had lain the frustration of Michael who should have and could have been there to help. They both knew he most likely would be there - but drinking in the study (the room he now favoured, ever since the night when he had been locked out of it and had tried to kick the door down) - just as he had been there every night since Octavian had arrived, just as he had been there every night while the rest of them had dinner in the kitchen.

It was only on his first night home that Octavian had asked, "Where's Dad?" and then had stopped Marinda's reply by remembering, "Oh, I forgot." He had drawn breath as if to comment further, but seemed to change his mind and the subject together and had not mentioned it again. Instead he had promised to cook pasta for Marinda and Heather one night.

"I'm a dab hand at that," he had confided with a wink and a wide theatrical smile. "Just wait till Seb and Sep and Julian are back - they'll die for it!"

Marinda's heart had warmed at the mention of her other temporarily forgotten children. She felt a twinge of guilt. Perhaps when they came back it would all be different, perhaps their life as a family was salvageable after all. Perhaps she had simply let her imagination run away with her and after the Retreat ...

And with the Retreat in mind she had arranged for another parent to collect Heather from school and drop her at home for the next four days, and she had persuaded Rosa to remain at the house until Octavian returned in the evening.

"Perhaps you could work in the afternoons next week instead of mornings," she had suggested, but Rosa had looked so alarmed at this that she had not pursued it, simply agreeing that Rosa could remain for the full day and telling her that, of course, she would be paid for the extra hours. It was all such an unnecessary complication when Michael would probably be at home himself, but it was the "probably" which drove her on. Even if she were certain of his presence he would almost certainly not be fit to drive; she had learned not to rely on him in any way.

It meant she had had to organize food as well, lunch for Rosa, dinner for Octavian and Heather. She knew Octavian was perfectly capable of cooking himself, yet he would be tired when he returned from RADA and she felt she should have possible menus available at the very least, and the same for Rosa, even though Rosa would not remain for dinner, and of course would have lunch alone.

She had also left snacks for Michael - all he ever seemed to eat these days, apart from the nightly slice of burned toast. She tried to ensure the snacks were as nutritious as possible - cheeses and nuts, which she tried not to make obvious were for him. He would not have liked that. If she had had time she would have prepared an avocado dip to leave in the fridge, one with carrot and celery sticks; he would have seen it when he filled the ice bucket and might have eaten something like that unthinkingly while he drank, and it would have been nourishing.

With a start she realized she was performing a small charade of little wifely duties and wondered why. She thought of Octavian and his acting theory - what was it? - that emotion would follow the motion. That if you feigned smiles and laughter your mood would actually lighten; that short breaths and clenched fists themselves could precipitate anger. Then doing these simple things for Michael could lead to genuine caring? Or was there caring first which led to the simple things? She wondered at the connection between pity and love, the connection between hate and love, or if there were any connection at all. She did not wonder about the connection between her last visit to the monastery and her current actions. She was too tired to think it through.

It had been a lot to arrange for a mere four days away. She had even had to remember to organize the laundry collection for Wednesday afternoon, leaving a last minute note for Rosa.

And so she arrived exhausted for the Retreat, feeling depleted and empty of all resources.

XIV

It was of course another world. There were twelve of them on the Retreat, eight men and four women, but apart from that first evening they did not speak. Even then it was only perfunctory, a hushed query about the time, an "Excuse me," as someone stepped in front of someone else.

City types, Brother Thaddeus had defined them. Marinda wondered idly which woman was the solicitor but it was impossible to tell; both men and women were dressed casually, several in jeans, one in a tracksuit. She herself was in a denim skirt and ivory blouse; the skirt had large pockets because she had not wanted to bring a handbag, although like the others she had packed a small holdall with toilet articles and a change of clothes. This she still carried as they moved in the direction of the ground floor chapel, herded by the old, furry Brother Aidan, smiling benignly as he pointed the way through his geraniums.

"What about this?" one of the men asked, raising his overnight bag, but the old monk merely nodded and pointed again towards the chapel.

"Later," came the dry rasping voice in afterthought as the man disappeared through the door.

The rest of them carried their belongings into the chapel, nodded to the cross on the altar and sat rather awkwardly together on the stone pews. One of the younger Brothers was waiting to address them.

"Hello, I'm Brother Thaddeus," he began, "your

Retreat Co-ordinator."

Marinda marvelled at his professional ease, having seen him before only in the tentative transposition of a son. Watching him more objectively now, he reminded her of a likeable squirrel, with his bushy rust-coloured hair, eager face and prominent teeth. A squirrel in Holy Orders, of course. She bit her lip, a little ashamed of her irreverence.

"For those of you who haven't been here before, I'm just going to tell you a little about what to expect," he continued. "When you get to your room you'll find a card like this one with our Rules and Instructions on it."

He brandished it above his head and now Marinda was reminded of an airline steward (but again in the black habit of Holy Orders) announcing safety instructions before take-off, what to do if the plane should shudder, fail, and nosedive towards the earth from whence it came, ashes to ashes. A touch of her old panic returned. What if it did fall, fail, this whole Retreat business? Then what would she do? Where was she hoping to fly to, anyway - heaven? Perhaps she was expecting too much.

She reminded herself that this was not the Curé D'Ars facing her now, that long dead sainted priest she had met once in a painting, where he stood famously telling the peasant of whom he had just asked directions, 'You have shown me the way to Ars; now I will show you the way to heaven.' No, it was only Brother Thaddeus and his directions were instructions for the Retreat itself, immediate and concrete. And the Retreat wouldn't, couldn't fail.

She had touched on the nature of forgiveness here before, had come so close to meaning, ultimate meaning, that thing the poets and philosophers called Truth; she knew it was here if she could only concentrate, learn, listen .... yes. She would listen and she would learn, and she would return with her garnered grace and wisdom to forgive Michael and they would dwell in harmony with their progeny while she covered her canvases with Truth and Beauty, imparting to all others the nature of forgiving ... for that was her quest. She forced her eyes back into focus on Brother Thaddeus.

"- giving your schedule and other bits of information like directions to the nearest loo. You will join us for meals in the refectory and for all the services here in the chapel. The addresses, there will be three a day of about twenty minutes each, they will also be given here. And you're really lucky," he added, lowering his voice and breaking into a boyish grin, "because Father Swithin is your Retreat Conductor and he's as good as they come."

Then more seriously he continued, "As you leave now, I'm going to ask you to check this list and tick off your own name and then write after it the name of the Brother you'd like to have for your Spiritual Director while you're here. You'll be meeting him twice a day and he's the one you'll make your confession to. If you don't have a preference or don't know any of us, we'll assign a Brother to you. After that I'll give you a card with the number of your room on it. Oh - one other thing. Our Retreats are held in silence, which starts with Compline this evening. Does anybody have any questions?"

Nobody had. The silence might already have begun since there was no sound other than the clearing of throats, occasional cough or scraping of shoes as they rose and headed towards the lectern where Brother Thaddeus was standing with the various papers.

"I wish you luck," he said to them. "It's hard work - and even a little scary - when you know you're coming face to face with God." He looked at them with anxious compassion as they approached, as if he truly cared about them but was uncertain of their survival. It was the way he had looked at the deer.

Marinda queued with the others to find her name, waiting in line behind a curly-haired man in a light anorak. What was he, she wondered, banker, company director, clerk? And what had brought him from the financial mile of the City to the Godfathers in this unlikely place? She realized she would never know. Nor was it any of her business.

When her turn came for the ballpoint pen she flicked a mark beside M LAWSON, then wrote Brother David's name under the heading for Spiritual Director. She noticed someone else had done the same. Then she collected the card for her room, number 4, and filed out of the chapel into the conservatory. Brother Aidan, still smiling, pointed the way to the wide hallway she remembered. She nodded to him, walking with others holding their own cards past the now familiar desk at the beginning of the hall. She soon found her room on the right.

It was small, no more than eight feet by ten and it held a single bed with a white cotton duvet, a table with a single drawer and a chair. The floor was covered with brown tiles; the walls were painted white. As Brother Thaddeus had indicated, a card with RULES AND INSTRUCTIONS FOR GUESTS was pinned to the back of the door. The only other objects in the room were a Bible, and a crucifix on the wall. There was a small window, however, which denied and undid the otherwise spartan simplicity of the room, for it hung like a painting on the wall, framing a flower garden which even in the dusk glowed with rich, luxuriant colours, red, gold, and orange. She thought of her palette and brush.

Slipping her holdall underneath the bed, she noticed the edge of a small thin mat and pulling it out, saw it was covered with worn green leather. A prayer mat, she reflected, oddly pleased. She knelt on it and folded her hands. But she did not know what to say.

* * * * *

"And furthermore I think Brother Thaddeus looks like a squirrel, which I know is irreverent."

Brother David threw back his head and laughed. There were fillings in his back teeth, not diamond fillings nor even gold, but the simple dark amalgam fillings which any ordinary 20th century mortal might be expected to have.

"Not irreverent," he said. "Irrelevant."

"Then thoughts aren't sins?"

He shook his head, still grinning. "They can be, of course they can - envy or greed or hatred or lust - if dwelt upon or acted upon. Your thought - your rather apt description (he smiled again) - was neither deliberate nor cruel, nor, I suspect, do you intend to use it as a satirical label in gossip, nor as a taunt."

It was the morning of the first day, after Mattins, after Mass, after the silent breakfast in the refectory with the twenty monks and eleven other retreatants and now she was with Brother David himself, sitting again in the small room where they had first spoken two weeks ago. Now, as then, he faced her straddling his chair. Perhaps that was his favourite position for confrontation. For now, as then, that felt like what it was. She was aware of power in the room, a giant held-back strength, and she felt defensive.

They were speaking of Confession. His first words to her had been to ask when she wanted to make it. She had quailed.

"But I've never made one. I don't know how."

"Ah. Then that will seem a great hurdle at first."

"Is it mandatory? Do I have to?"

"No."

She was surprised. "But you advise it?"

"Yes."

"Why?"

"So that we become aware of sin itself. Once we name our sins we can no longer pretend they don't exist. Nor excuse them."

"That's a novel approach," she said slowly, "one I suppose they would call politically incorrect." For somewhere in another world someone with horn-rimmed glasses had said there was always a reason for bad behaviour, meaning - she could see it now - the reason became the cause became the excuse. In that world there was no sin at all. It was an idea which was appealing - but false. She knew deep down it simply was not true. Michael could not escape so easily.

"Very perceptive," the monk nodded. "The concept of sin itself is certainly politically incorrect. So is evil. And so is death. These are the obscenities in the world today, the unsayable things. Not sex, which used to be the shocker at the dinner table - although that is still what most people think is meant by sin."

His words surprised her, implying conversant awareness of smart dinner parties and conversaziones in direct contrast with the silence and frugal meals she had shared with the Godfathers. She wondered how he knew these things. If she had asked, would he merely have said he was not born in a monastery? Or perhaps he had simply learned from those who came to the confessional. It was a sobering thought, that confessional.

"Well, I don't think of sex as sin," she said, "necessarily. Except sometimes to wonder how the most beautiful thing in the world can turn into the ugliest without love." She could not escape the shadow of Michael.

"Well, you've said it, haven't you?"

It was strange to be having this easy conversation with a monk and yet oddly natural, too, sexual connotation having been traded for sexual concept, transcending the usual subtle gender games for the clarity and purity of thought. One of the surprising freedoms of celibacy, perhaps, now extending its aura even to her.

"But we're digressing from the idea of the confessional where we do not name our sins to excuse them."

"I get the point," she continued with a sigh, thinking of alcohol and Michael's many sins. "It's responsibility, isn't it? Because after we name our sins presumably we can do something about them, right?" But Michael would never name his. He would never even admit he carried any, probably genuinely believed he had never committed any. A pity she couldn't list them for him. Ha! The list would cover a roll of loo paper. But what good would it do?

"Partly right. Amendment is something. Atonement is something else."

She thought of her red-eyed husband and the damaged door, pictured the eyes clear and the door panels replaced. It would take no more than a carpenter and a few drops of Optrex. Amendment. But Atonement? Isn't that after all what she wanted, total reconciliation for herself with Michael and for Michael to be reconciled with life and yes, perhaps even with God again; the splintered door and the red eyes not just patched up and repaired but made perfect as once they both had been, recreated in reconciliation? Was it possible?

Memory, an old black and white film unreeling, stirred, blurred pictures shot through with slivers of silver light, a long lost Michael with his head thrown back, laughing ... Was that possible?

"I didn't really come here for all this emphasis on sin. Is that what it's all about, is your Order sin-centred?"

The monk laughed with undiluted amusement. "No. A clever way of putting it, but wrong absolutely. We're God-centred. But before we approach God's table we wash our hands, that's all. I'm merely suggesting soap and water."

"I see."

"You say you didn't come for this. Then why did you come?"

"You told me to."

He nodded. "Indeed."

"And I came to learn about forgiving, about the nature of forgiveness. Because that would be the key to my life, I think, the locked-in locked-up mess of my marriage."

"Why? You think by learning to forgive your husband you will live happily ever after?"

"Perhaps something like that."

"Then perhaps your quest is centred on self."

"But I don't understand. It's for him, too. Talk to me about forgiveness."

"We are talking about it."

"We are? Then I didn't know it. Last time I knew it, when you gave me your definition of forgiveness."

"I remember."

"You said it was seeing somebody - the unforgiven - as God intended him to be." Oh surely it wasn't just a quest for her own benefit, somewhere deep inside she wanted to forgive Michael for his own sake, and beyond that for the sake of a kind of order, a goodness barely glimpsed, golden and divine. "I would like to do that," she said slowly, "see Michael that way. I'm just not sure I can, or how to go about doing it. There must be something more. But that's not what we're talking about now, is it?"

"In a roundabout way it is, yes. There's nothing more. We're taking the first step in that direction. You're concerned with forgiving your husband, yes?"

"Yes."

"We will come to that. But first we will speak of God's forgiveness. Confession. Absolution."

There it was again - Confession. But Confession means dragging up the past. Wouldn't it be better to learn to forgive, if I can figure out how to accomplish that, and then to forget and go on from there?"

"No. Real forgiving is part of not forgetting. God doesn't forget your sins but loves you in spite of them. You may learn to give, forgive, without Confession. Can you receive forgiveness without Confession?"

"You mean without asking for it, because that seems to be what Confession is. Asking by acknowledgment. I don't know. Maybe not." Could she forgive Michael if he didn't ask for it, want it, even acknowledge that he needed it? Could God? "As for me, can't I confess alone to God?"

"Of course you can. But would you? Do you?"

She made no reply in her confusion.

"And who would absolve the unnamed, unacknowledged sin?"

"Absolve?" She was in full retreat now, forced back on her own shortcomings, not Michael's. "I only meant - it seems wrong - not wrong, maybe just unwise - to drag things up that are over now, gone. Isn't it couldn't it, wouldn't it be better to let sleeping dogs lie? Die?"

"But as you say, they aren't dead. An unnamed sin smoulders, hidden away, forgotten. Much better to bring it out, baptise it, transform it."

Baptise a sin? Wasn't that heresy?

"And then, and only then," he continued softly, "can we give it away. Set it free."

At Marinda's look of incredulity he merely lifted his

index finger skyward in a barely perceptible movement reminiscent of a bidder at Christie's.

"I myself have never felt cleaner - or freer -" he added softly, "than after my first Confession."

"Well, I suppose I could try it" she said hesitantly, still thinking how much easier it would be to list Michael's sins than her own. "As a matter of discipline."

"Good. Shall we say half an hour before Compline? In the Lady Chapel."

"But -" She felt frantically unprepared. "But I won't know where to begin. Am I supposed to cover my whole life? In half an hour?"

"More or less. Don't give me a spiritual autobiography. Try dividing your life into five-year sections. You can use the seven deadly sins as markers. Don't worry if you can't remember things. Sins genuinely forgotten are forgiven through intention. And don't qualify. If you hit your brother when you were ten - or twenty - say so, don't tell me why he deserved it. God already knows all that. It's your sins he wants, not your brother's."

Guiltily she wondered if he knew what she had been thinking about Michael's sins.

"I'm sure you've heard," he said, slinging his leg over the chair as he stood up to indicate their time was over, "that anything said in the confessional is inviolate. That is true."

"You won't tell, is that it? Not even the police if I confessed to murdering Michael?"

"Not even the police if you confessed to murdering Michael," he repeated evenly. His dark eyes locked swiftly onto her own. "But you haven't, have you?" he asked half mockingly.

* * * * *

No, she hadn't. Nor, she began to realize, had she been so worried about that particular matter since she had last seen the Brother David. She did not mention the possible connection between the two facts but a hazy realization was forming that perhaps there might be one. She wondered if the monk would ever again place his hands on her head and pray in tongues. She wished he would but he certainly did not seem so inclined today.

Still, he had said they would speak about her forgiving Michael, that there would be time. That was his intention and hers, too, and both of them truly believed at that moment that there really would be time.

XV

By Wednesday evening Marinda had adjusted enough to her new surroundings to imagine herself a nun. She began to feel she had always been in this timeless place, surrounded by the peace and serenity of these brothers.

Her other life seemed to belong to someone else, the big old house in Barnes, the husband, the five faces of children, filed away like fading photographs in an album from a distant past. Yet these had been her life, her touchstones of reality, and as such had defined her own being. Before now she would not have been sure she could or would exist without them, and yet they now seemed indescribably far away. Was that what happened in death, she wondered, this letting go, this merging, submerging, of the sharp outlines of reality as you stepped into another dimension?

For that was what she seemed to have done here, however inadvertently or temporarily. The Godfathers lived in a different concept of time altogether, another dimension; however their days might seem divided and ruled by bells and offices said or sung, their gaze was directed straight through the window of eternity and it did not frighten them. They truly believed there was a point in time when the Creator of the universe had entered his own creation, fusing all dimensions forever into spectacular truth. And so they were able to live in a different way, these black-robed men, and it was a way more seductive than she could have believed possible.

How easy it was to step into their ordered life, the offices, the meditations. Meal times she liked especially, when each of them collected a simple bowl of soup and sat at one of the long wooden tables set out with loaves of brown bread. At lunch they ate in silence; at supper one of the Brothers read aloud, not from scripture, as she would have expected, but surprisingly from Tolkien. The idyll was only marred by one of the brothers noisily and wetly slurping soup through the gaps in his front teeth, but not even this could fully distract from, detract from, the spirit of camaraderie - no, of love - which lingered over the brothers and which seemed to extend to the retreatants as well, perhaps even to all other things.

Their inner peace was palpable. They seemed to have a joy in living itself, a delight in the most simple, the most basic things, the warmth of their meal, the fact of their visitors. Were these the things which comprised the love of God?

Marinda loved it all. She loved her little room with its view of the flower garden, rich and wild with colour, and she loved the silence and tranquillity that was waiting there whenever she returned to it. And partly she loved it because she knew it was temporary.

Her Confession had gone well; faced with the immediacy of having to do it she had managed to lump her life's wrongdoings into twenty minutes of notes which she then read out on her knees to the silent silhouette of Brother David on the other side of the grille.

And he had been right, after his absolution and his blessing she had been lightheaded with relief and a kind of joy - though this was mitigated by surprise when he told her that daily Confession was desirable during Retreats, adding as well that "The first Confession is never as important as the second."

Oh no. Denial was still an automatic reflex, although she began to understand the reasoning behind his statement late that night as she observed and reviewed her actions of the day, her hasty steps towards the loo in order to reach it before a slower retreatant, her secret annoyance with the Brother who had slurped his soup. A new awareness of the small things was being instilled almost imperceptibly into her thinking, along with the great awakening awareness of Pride, that inescapable pinnacle of sin which surfaced even as she confessed it, pride in naming pride. It was a different world and she was moving in it awkwardly, like a child learning to take its first steps.

Sloth. What was that all about? It had puzzled her as she skimmed the seven sins; she had a momentary picture of herself hanging lazily upside down in a tree, drowsing when she ought to have been collecting Heather from school - until Brother David in one of their discussions explained the nature of accidie. And then she remembered the blank canvases and unused brushes in her studio, remembered her own talent, as a gift tossed carelessly into a corner to lie perpetually half unwrapped, half untapped. accidie. Confession to make us aware of sin, Brother David had said. How right he was. But she had never realized how many things could bear that label. And yet there was a lightness in that realization, too, a simple satisfaction in knowing that accidie and sins in general could be made to fade and disappear.

She had a sudden vision of an endless stairway leading to perfection. She could never climb it herself, she knew that, for the steps were slippery as ice. But she knew the staircase was there, she could see it, and perhaps one day she could even paint it. She imagined it on a canvas hanging somewhere in a gallery, a frozen stairway delicate as spun glass, its icy tracery stretching skyward, endless and impossible in the moonlight. Perfection. Cobalt blue, titanium white.

She was no longer thinking in terms of Michael's sins.

*****

"I think I should have been a nun," she told Brother David Thursday at their daily meeting.

"Why?" His features did not move though she sensed a smile.

"It's a good life."

"You see only the surface."

"Nevertheless."

"And you see with the artist's eye, imagined and romanticized. Your own brand of reality."

"But isn't that what you have - your own brand of reality?"

He raised his eyebrows. "Perhaps."

"I know you can't be perfect, that there are probably currents of humanity running under what I see. But even so, life in this place, this particular monastery, seems like a calm sea, something constant and reassuring which doesn't change. It really appeals to me. The female equivalent, of course," she added with a wistful smile.

"You are misled." He spoke harshly now. "The waves of change are lapping against the walls even here, strong waves, the world's definition of reality. We are going to be divided soon by a tidal wave and some of us will drown. God is the only constant. You will never find unchange except in God, outside the finite, outside time. We are caught in the web of time, all of us. And it is too late for you to become a nun."

"Oh, I concede that. I just think perhaps I should have been."

"You would have needed a particular vocation."

"Perhaps I had one and didn't recognize it. How does one know?"

"One knows."

She imagined a recruiting poster showing the giant face of God, arm raised, finger pointing: I want YOU. She could have drawn such a poster. "I could have made a Vocation."

"And your children?"

"Would not have been."

"You would want that?"

"Now, having known them? I suppose not, no.." Through a cloud of guilt she tried to conjure up their faces. "It's just that here they seem so far away, unreal. It's possible to imagine them somewhere else, belonging to someone else ...," her voice trailed away. "But to wish them unborn -," she began to sense the proximity of unforgivable sin. "Oh, no." Sebastian's cheeky face broke through her thoughts with startling clarity and she was saved. "Definitely not. I was only imagining what it might have been like."

"That's not the way it works. You didn't have a vocation to be a religious, so what?" There was an edge of irritation now in his voice. "It's pointless to map the roads not followed. Imagination can be your enemy, regret an indulgence. Did you ever play Whist?"

"A little. Once." The question surprised her. "I didn't like it much."

He shook his head impatiently as if to indicate that didn't matter, that she was missing the point. "We're all dealt a certain hand of cards in life. Some are good, some not so good. I don't know why, because I don't happen to know the mind of God. Some cards we are allowed to choose. But what cards we hold - and they're all different from each other's - is never so important as how we play them. You're querying the given, the initial deal. You can't do that."

"Michael was dealt to me?"

"Michael was one of the cards you chose."

"Damn. Sorry, that just slipped out. And now I have to deal with him?"

"That doesn't mean you control him. He has free will, too."

"It's an awful situation."

"The situation is your hand of cards."

"Damn!"

"But you hold some winners, too, Intelligence, for a start."

"A given?"

He nodded.

"Not a chosen, like Michael," she mused slowly. "But when you choose a card in Whist, it's more chance than choice. You're not allowed to know what it is - you only hope it's a good one, the right one."

His look of surprise was followed by laughter. "Touché! The image breaks down, at least for my own illustration. It wasn't a very good one anyway."

With amazing generosity of spirit he seemed genuinely delighted to have been caught out. How many things she was learning in these conversations, among them that Brother David himself was not infallible. She felt she was being given insights, like tools, to work with later on, was being allowed to speak with a man whose integrity was unassailable and shaped by total goodness.

These few days on the Retreat were priceless days, she knew it even then. Perhaps they had been given to her as extra cards from which to draw. As Grace.

* * * * *

Father Swithin's talks to the group were electrifying, better than TV, accompanied always by the little clicks of his mechanical elbows locking into place as he gestured or moved his papers. He seemed to control his hooks with the muscles of his back and shoulders; almost imperceptibly he shrugged and nudged and shifted to make them move.

Of all the monks Marinda thought he seemed the happiest, the most secure, sure and serene. She could see why he was the Father Superior. And yet he was not allowed to celebrate the Mass, for when she had expressed initial disappointment that it was another priest/brother who elevated the host that first morning, Brother David had told her that Brother Swithin was prevented from doing so by the Archbishop himself.

"It was felt the Host or chalice might be dropped," he

explained.

"But he's in perfect control!"

Brother David shrugged.

"How disappointed he must have been."

"Perhaps. If so, he transformed the disappointment into something else."

"Can you really do that?"

"Yes."

How, oh how? She approached the lectures full of awe, feeling anything the small man said would be full of wisdom. And because she was looking for it, she found it.

Father Swithin laughed frequently during his talks so that they, the retreatants, laughed, too, and gradually forgot his appalling disability. On Thursday he spoke of prayer, defining it simply as touching God. "A reaching out, "he said, extending the claw at the end of his rod-like arm, "to make contact. To touch ..."

(She thought of the ceiling of the Sistine Chapel, the hand of God touching the hand of Adam in the very act of creation itself. How poignant that out of all the senses Brother Swithin should choose to speak of touch.)

" ... not necessarily with the crudity of request, not even with definitions of praise, although these are certainly forms of prayer, but the immediacy of touch itself -" and here he extended both metal rods with their hooks upturned, "-saying, I am here." The light glinted on his steel and glanced off his round bald head, momentarily making him look for all the world like a miniature robot.

And yet the eyes were human, fully so, not even the glass shields in front of them, protective magnifiers, could conceal that. He looked at them, his audience, with knowledge and intense compassion as he continued speaking in a quiet metallic voice. "We can do that at any time, reach out to touch the hand of God. It is always there, outstretched (the Sistine Chapel again) and waiting. If we reach, contact is made - always - whether we feel it or not. (So the metal claws, now closing and withdrawing, were an illustration after all). Think on this."

It was good stuff and it was only the beginning; she would write it all down when she got back to her room later. She knew from his other talks that he would lead them through subsequent elaborations and unexplored avenues of thought well worthy of remembrance and reflection. Right now she did not want to make notes the way one or two of the others were doing; she did not want to lose sight of the man himself, this astonishing example, this paragon of forgiveness and love. That, too, was worthy of study and reflection, of writing down.

She fully intended to do just that and perhaps she actually would have done so, but already there was a whisper of disturbance somewhere in the depths of the building, the sense of an unseen, unheard quiver of disorder in the air.

As they filed from the chapel in silence, Brother David suddenly appeared beside her, his hand surprisingly on her elbow, guiding her through the geraniums to the reception desk in the wide inner hall.

In the small office beyond she could see Brother Thaddeus and Octavian standing together, waiting.

XVI

"What is it? What's wrong?"

It was her own voice but it seemed to come from a long way off, muffled, dream-like, unreal. And that was appropriate for she seemed to be in a trance, seemed to be witnessing a tableaux where time itself was standing still, non-existent, the faces facing her locked in the mirror of eternity.

She wanted it to be so, this moment, wanted it never to move, knowing that when it did it would bring with it some terrible knowledge, some consequence that would change her life forever. Yet if the moment were halted now it would not, could not happen, time would disappear, be held in eternal equilibrium, tense dissolving in tension. She tried not to breathe, willed her heart to stop beating.

How pale Octavian was, unsmiling. Pale, too, was Brother Thaddeus, frightened beside him, no, not frightened but with a suppressed excitement in his manner she had not seen before, not even at the scene of the dying deer. In a flash of intuition she recognized the sameness she had sensed in each of them before, a similarity she would neither name nor face, not now, perhaps not ever. It was not what had brought them together here in this place now. What had?

"Mum, you need to come home," her first-born spoke gently, too gently, as if she were very old. "Something has happened."

"Has someone died?" Her mouth was so dry she

sounded like Michael in an advanced stage of drinking, her tongue sticking painfully to the roof of her mouth with every word.

But he shook his head. "I'll explain in the car."

She accepted this without question. "I'll get my things."

She moved then, shattering the tableaux, walking away from it hurriedly to confront her small white room for the final time. A wave of peace flowed out from it as she opened the door, so palpable and strong it almost knocked her down before receding, leaving the cell empty behind it, drained and unfamiliar. Whatever peace and meaning she had found within those walls was gone now.

And this will be the world's quickest packing job, she thought with the part of her mind still functioning, tipping the contents of the single drawer into her holdall and grabbing her jacket from the hook on the door.

"I'm ready," she said to the three men waiting beside the desk.

Octavian nodded and took the holdall, Brother Thaddeus was looking anxiously at Octavian, only Brother David met her eyes as he made a quick sign of the cross in her direction.

"Go with God's blessing," he said quietly.

He must know what it was about, must have been told. There was so much that needed to be said but she could not reach out to him now, could only manage, "I'm sorry," and the look of a person drowning as she followed Octavian through the door.

* * * * *

"So what is it?" she asked in the car.

They were in the park again, surprisingly it was mid-afternoon (not night as it should have been), the time when the sunlight slanted with unbearable sadness across the earth. It must have rained earlier, and heavily, for the land was wet and the light glanced off surfaces everywhere with the piercing brightness of shattered mirrors. There must have been high winds as well for here and there a large branch had been ripped off a tree and lay with glistening leaves on the ground. Octavian was driving badly, narrowly missing one car, alternately slowing and accelerating without reason.

"I don't know how to tell you. It's Heather."

"Tell me."

"She's with the Fishers."

"Why? If she's ill why isn't she home? I left her at home with Rosa. And you. And Michael."

"It was - Rosa's idea - for her to go there."

"After school?" Why was she having to coax every word out of him? Why were they talking like this? Why didn't he tell her what had happened, why was it taking so long? She wanted to scream and in a fury of frustration turned to him, then stopped at the sight of his tortured face.

"She didn't go to school today. Rosa took her to the Fishers instead."

"She couldn't have. Susan has a bad ankle, she's even had to send Judy to stay somewhere. If Heather was sick Rosa should have looked after her or rung the doctor, and anyway -" She was playing for time and she knew it, anything to prolong, postpone what he was going to say.

"She wasn't exactly sick." His words were reluctant and slow, as if he were translating a foreign tongue.

There was a sudden jolt as the car swiped one of the wooden stakes lining the road, then moved back again.

"For God's sake, Octavian, tell me what you mean, tell me what's happening!"

He gripped the steering wheel with chalk-white fingers before speaking in a voice so low she could barely make out the words.

"Rosa thinks - Dad has been doing something to Heather."

"Oh my God." She did not misunderstand. "Oh my God." Awareness was instantaneous as the unspeakable horror of his words began to sink in through layer after layer of shock and recognition. "Oh my God."

For a second her mind slipped into another dimension where she was standing on a white sand shore, watching a ship with golden sails, a delicate ship from a fairy tale, skimming the glittering surface of an enchanted sea. From somewhere far away the notes of a lute blew high and clear on the wind, irresistibly beautiful, filling the golden sails with sound. Then even as she watched, the music changed, crashed into a hideous cacophony of sound as the ship was sucked doomed and drowning into a monstrous whirlpool, black, chaotic, the kind of thing that did not belong in a fairy tale at all but in a Greek tragedy. It could not happen in such a place with the white sand shore and the enchanted sea, it was wrong, things were out of kilter. The stories had become crossed, the tales tangled, the colours mixed, no longer gold and silver, the music lost; all was lost, all was wrong, the world was out of kilter.

It could not be true. What Octavian had told her could not be true.

It could not be true and yet a dozen little signs were beginning to surface now in the murky water of her mind, like flotsam floating in the sea, debris bubbling to the surface after a shipwreck. The child's nightmares. The reluctance to stay at home. The avoidance of her father. Of course.

"Rosa told you this?"

"Yes."

"Where is Rosa now?"

"At home. Ours. At least she was when I left. I asked her to wait for us - for you. I came back early after filming. The tea commercial, remember?" he laughed bitterly. "We've started already, much sooner than I thought."

"And Rosa told you?" she repeated. That in itself was scarcely credible.

He nodded. "Rosa's in a very bad way." Then barely audibly he added, "So am I."

"And Susan. She told Susan, too?"

"I don't know what Rosa told her. She'd have had to tell her something."

Then at last she asked the question waiting to be asked. "Where is your father?" She could not bring herself to use his name.

"I'm not sure. Rosa said he'd gone to the Garrick for lunch. Anyway he wasn't there when I left. I came straight to get you."

"Then all you know is what Rosa told you." And Rosa might have lied, might have made the whole thing up, might have been mistaken, might have had a complete and sudden overwhelming breakdown or been possessed by an evil spirit, might have been sleepwalking - talking - or decided finally to sample the contents of the liquor cabinet herself or become temporarily insane ... oh surely there were many reasons why Rosa might have spoken as she did, if she did, many reasons other than the truth itself.

They drove in numb silence. Traffic was heavy in Priory Lane; it was the afternoon school run, there were the faces of children in several cars, the glimpse of blue and yellow school uniforms in an estate car ahead of them along with a dog in the back.

They drove on, skirting the first meadow of Barnes Common, then over the hump of the first level-crossing, only to stop at the second where the red lights were flashing with the barriers down.

"Mum - I'm sorry - but I think I've got to move out."

She nodded dumbly. Why discuss this now?

"Whatever happens I can't face him again."

"Heather. Loves you." It was a statement more than an appeal. The sense of abandonment was overwhelming.

"I'll still see her. Of course I will."

One train passed but still the gates did not lift; the red

lights went on flashing in the same tempo as the accelerated beating of her heart, sharp and painful as the ticking of a clock.

"I need to go soon. Now, really."

"Where?"

"I don't know. I thought - if you didn't mind - I'd talk to your monastery. Maybe they would let me have your room there for the rest of your Retreat. Just until I can think things out."

Incapable of speaking or even of thinking she could only look at him.

"Don't worry," he said, "please don't worry. Heather's okay now. She's been rescued."

Don't worry. The age-old meaningless reassurance. Heather's okay now. Heather would never be okay. How could she be?

Another train passed but still the barrier remained down.

"We've hit just the wrong time," he muttered. "When it lifts do I drive straight to Susan's?"

Yes, she would go to Susan's and would hold her child tightly, tightly, feel the spun gold hair against her cheek, tell her with the same meaningless reassurance that it was going to be all right. But no, she must see Rosa first, make sure, make absolutely sure - and how could it ever be all right again?

"No. Home."

"Then -" he hesitated. "Mum, is it all right if I just drop you? I can't go back in, I just can't."

Of course. It was her problem to deal with, not his. How could she ever have thought otherwise?

"And is it okay if I take the car? Just for tonight?"

She nodded dully to everything, aware that he had become a child again himself, as such was probably in need of her comfort and reassurance. She had none to give him. They could not comfort each other. A line from a bygone classroom passed through her head, John Donne maintaining somewhere in a poem that 'No man is an island'. But that was wrong, she thought, completely wrong. We are all islands. When the crunch comes we are all of us alone, islands encircled by the sea.

"I'll see that you get it back tomorrow."

What was he talking about? Oh yes, the car. He had asked to use the car. What did it matter? She wouldn't need it. Heather was at Susan's but she herself could easily walk to Susan's afterwards. After what? After speaking to Rosa.

A long line of traffic had built up in the Common behind them, awaiting the third train. The railway warning lights flashed on and off alternately, incessantly, in small sharp stabs of bright red pain.

XVII

For the seventh time Rosa walked from the kitchen to the hall to the dining room to the window. There she would peer through the white film of curtain to the gravel driveway, the street beyond, and the Common beyond that. She was waiting for the Senora's pearl-gray car, for Octavian to return with the Senora herself. But the drive remained empty and the street held only occasional passing cars. She could tell by the first hint of an approaching engine whether it was going to be the wrong one, going too fast to stop at this house. She would let three cars pass, then she would turn and walk back into the kitchen, passing the empty study on the way.

The Senor was not there. He had gone to his club for lunch. She knew he always did this on Thursdays and was more than glad when she heard the front door close behind him during what had become the worst morning of her life.

She did not know when he would return. Already it was four o'clock. Already Octavian had come back and she had told him the terrible thing and he had gone away again to fetch his mother. And he had asked her, Rosa, to wait, to stay, to tell his mother what she had already told him. She crossed herself, praying fervently they would arrive before the Senor did. She did not know how she could ever look at the Senor's face again.

She had not yet done so that day, looked at him. He was still in bed when she had arrived that morning; the door of the master bedroom had been closed. She knew about his insomnia because the Senora had sometimes mentioned it. She had explained to Rosa once about an actor's schedule, how because of their plays actors worked late and slept late and the habit was hard to break even when the plays dried up. Rosa thought the insomnia might be due to that. The Senora had said that sometimes when he could not sleep he would get up at four in the morning and wander about the house for an hour or so before going back to bed. Rosa knew about the sleeping pills in their bathroom cabinet, the level of which went down dramatically from time to time. So it had not seemed unusual today for him to remain in the bedroom until mid-morning.

Much later she had heard him in the drawing room, had heard the floorboards creaking from time to time through the ceiling as he moved about. And from time to time she had heard the tinkling notes of that sad little song in the cabinet with the whisky after he came down to the study. It was one of the mornings when he had no coffee.

Once he came to the door of the kitchen where she was working, but by then she already knew about the terrible thing and she turned her back, pretending not to know he was there. And after awhile with a grunt of disapproval he went away again and she could hear him climbing the stairs. Ha! To him it must have seemed like any other day. He did not know his daughter had not gone to school at all that day, did not know what she, Rosa, now knew. Nor, she thought now as she waited for the car, did he know the Senora was returning a day early from her Retreat.

Rosa's hands were black. She had altered the day's routine in a frantic flurry of activity and had taken out every piece of silver the Lawsons owned, spreading these about until the kitchen resembled Aladdin's cave with silver dishes, jugs, trays, cutlery, salvers and candelabra covering every available surface, including the floor. It was no wonder the Senor had snorted in disapproval as he turned away.

She polished furiously, her hands and nails ingrained with grime like a garage mechanic; she had purposefully and perversely left off her rubber gloves in a kind of penance for something she could not articulate but which had to do with the terrible thing. The harder she scrubbed, the less likely she was to think, that much she knew as she attacked and dented a delicate filigree bon-bon dish with a cloth soaked in Goddard's thick pink Long-Term-Silver-Polish. The sharp astringent smell pierced her nostrils. Small drops of perspiration formed on the charcoal down above her upper lip as she worked and there were large damp circles under the arms of her smock.

She would remain hunched in the same position for several moments, rubbing frantically in a circular motion, then suddenly she would stop and make the long trek to the dining room window again to look for the car. Nothing. She looked at her watch where the white gloves of Mickey Mouse were pointing to the big red numbers. It felt unnatural to be in this house in the afternoon when morning was her time, but of course she had promised that to the Senora. She wished the Senora would come. The Senora would know what to do.

She felt terrible. Her head ached and there was an awful, gnawing emptiness in the bottom of her stomach which she could neither define nor dispel, but which she wanted to go away. She wanted this morning to go away as well, but in spite of everything she kept remembering it, seeing again in flashes the terrible thing she had seen this morning.

Yesterday had been so different. She had arrived early at the house as Senora Marinda had suggested; she was there by 7:30 (the bus had been crowded but traffic was light, they had sped across the bridge and down the long avenue of Castlenau) in time for her to oversee Heather's departure for school a few minutes later with her brother. Octavian had been in high spirits.

"We've had a cereal-eating contest, Rosa," he had announced, "which I'm afraid my sister won." And somewhat embarrassed, he had indicated the kitchen table which was littered with corn-flakes and coco-pops.

"It is no matter," Rosa had smiled, for she did not mind extra work where the children were concerned.

"It was the only way I could get her to eat breakfast at all," Octavian had explained as the little girl was clinging to his sweater, her face hidden in its folds in an attitude which had not seemed unusual at the time. Their father had not yet come downstairs.

"But I think her shirt is yesterday's," Rosa had said, noting the smudged creases on the back of the canary-yellow cotton.

"Oops!" Octavian had looked sheepish, Heather's face still buried in his side. "Guess I should have checked that."

"Wait, I bring another!" Rosa had run upstairs to the child's room, pleased to be useful, knowing four other yellow shirts were hanging in the closet where she herself had placed them, freshly ironed, the day before.

The change was quickly made; the two had gone, and Rosa herself had gone happily into the kitchen for her coffee before attacking the cleaning. Yesterday.

All that day she had hummed as she worked, glad to be in this house in London with this famous man and his perfect family, her family. Of course she was grateful for her brother Juan as well and her sister-in-law and nephews and nieces, but they existed almost as extensions of herself, as sounding boards for her life with the Lawsons. And while they might not have been as fascinated as she was by her adopted family, they listened patiently and courteously as she talked about them while helping to prepare the evening meal, or during the commercial breaks when they were gathered around the TV.

She had been thinking that soon there would be even more to tell, for soon it would be Christmas and all the Lawson children would be home again, Septimus back from America, Julian and Sebastian home from Harrow and Eton. It was very good to have Octavian living at home once more and she hoped that Heather would never have to leave at all. Sometimes the English did not send their daughters away to boarding school even when they sent their sons, she had learned that. There was no denying Rosa liked it better when the house was full, even though it meant more work for her. But it also meant there was more to tell her brother and his family in Acton.

She had told them about the Senora being away now and that she would be working full days at the Lawsons for a week, afternoons as well as mornings, but she had had difficulty explaining the Retreat, mostly because she did not understand it herself.

But the time had gone well through yesterday. Yesterday morning had been the same as ever, and at lunchtime she had set a single place in the dining room for the Senor and had placed an avocado stuffed with prawns on the table, together with some brown bread and butter and a bottle of chilled white wine, all just as the Senora had directed. The Senora had told her not to worry if he didn't eat, adding that sometimes he didn't. Rosa did not question this.

The Senor had been sitting at the desk in the study, surrounded by photographs; she could see him plainly through the open door, but instinctively and shyly she had knocked on the doorframe and waited for him to look up before saying, "Your lunch, she is in the dining room, Senor."

He had nodded, without looking at her, and she had hastened back into the kitchen herself, to eat her own avocado. She did not like avocadoes, nor did she like prawns, but the Senora would not have known that and it was the Senora who had arranged the menu for both of them to eat the same thing. Normally, of course, she would have finished work and left the house by then.

But she had stayed on through yesterday afternoon, just as she had the day before that, doing the ironing and re-arranging the linen cupboard. Later one of the school mothers, flushed and frustrated, had rung the doorbell with Heather in tow.

"The silly girl wouldn't come to the door by herself," the woman had complained. "She didn't even want to get out of the car."

"Gracias, senora," Rosa had replied, taking refuge in her own language at this hint of criticism of one of her beloved children, taking Heather's hand firmly from the woman's grasp, noticing the estate car full of children which was double-parked in the background with its engine running.

Once back inside, she had made a piece of cinnamon toast for Heather and the child had sat pale and solemn at the kitchen table toying with it and sipping at a glass of milk. But when Rosa stepped briefly into the utility room to unload the tumble-dryer, she had bumped into the little girl as she turned around with a startled gasp of surprise, for the child had followed her as close and silent as a shadow.

"Come," the Spanish woman had said kindly with her arms full of towels, "we fold these on the kitchen table."

Obediently and silently the child had returned with her to the table, her small hands smoothing and patting the towels in imitation of the older woman. Then she had returned without interest to the milk and toast, while Rosa marvelled wistfully that she should miss her mother so much after only two days.

"Is there homework?" Rosa had asked tentatively.

And she remembered how, with a look almost of relief, the little girl had run to the hallway to retrieve her school satchel, and opening it, had taken out a pencil case and workbook. Perhaps this was what always happened in the afternoons, Rosa had thought, here at the kitchen table. She did not know.

Not long after that Octavian had arrived and the child had clung tightly to him as he laughingly tried to remove his coat.

Rosa had left them then, satisfied with her day, sure

that her family was functioning as it should and looking forward to tomorrow.

But all that was yesterday.

This morning it had been raining heavily and there were gale force winds; the bus had had to detour around a big old oak tree which had blown down in Castlenau. Nevertheless she had again arrived at seven-thirty, almost literally blowing in the door, where she was met in the hall by a frantic, harassed Octavian.

"Thank God you're here, Rosa, maybe you can help. Heather isn't dressed yet, I can't even get her out of her room, I don't know what's the matter with her, but I've got to be on time this morning of all mornings, it's the first day of filming and - I don't know what I'm going to do! Why is she doing this? This is no time for hide-and-seek!" He spread his arms in desperation, started up the stairs, then turned and ran back down again. "I've tried everything but I just haven't got time - do you think you could get her ready? And call somebody else to take her to school, Susan Fisher or one of -"

Rosa held up thickened hands, palms out. "Do not worry." This was Octavian, her Octavian, whom she had known since he was seven, and he was turning to her for help. A massive surge of warmth coursed through her body, reinforcing her strength and determination. "Do not worry," she repeated. "You go, I take care of things." A brilliant idea occurred to her. "The Senor must take her to school."

The sudden relief on Octavian's face gladdened her heart but even then she was surprised by his surprise at the mention of his father. Why had he not thought of that himself? Her sister-in-law would have lost no time in turning Juan bodily out of bed in a similar situation. But her thoughts were cut off by the young man's hug of gratitude.

"Rosa, you're a one-off," he cried, "you really are! Thanks a million - See you later!" Grabbing his umbrella and opening the door with an "It's supposed to clear up later!", he was gone.

Rosa's cup of happiness was indeed brimful, spilling out and running over like the rain pouring down the windows outside, as she mounted the stairs on sturdy legs. It was the second hug she had had from the Lawsons in a week. She could not remember such a thing happening since the children were very small.

The door to the master bedroom was closed but she would deal with the child first. The door to that bedroom was open although the child was not in sight.

"Heather?" She stepped inside the room, stocky and determined. She had told Octavian she would manage and manage she would, but now for the first time she was beginning to feel unease at the oddness of the situation.

The bed was rumpled, the pink eiderdown pulled up, but it did not look as if the child was there. Stuffed animals and dolls watched her in silence from the white bookshelves lining the walls. The white sliding doors of the closet were closed. The small white chair with its pink cushion stood empty beside the white desk.

She swivelled suddenly in her tracks as a new possibility occurred to her - but no, the door of the bathroom across the hall was standing open and she could see that it, too, was empty.

She turned back to the bed, knowing from a thousand hooverings there would be enough room for a child to be hiding underneath it.

"Heather?"

She dropped on all fours and lifted the valance but saw only a Barbie doll and one fluffy pink slipper. She stood up again, looked again at the bed, and was puzzled.

The eiderdown was rumpled and lumpy, but the biggest lump was still not big enough to conceal a child. Or was it? She seized one satin corner and hastily pulled the whole thing down. The bottom sheet was covered in blood.

"Madre de Dios!"

A faint sound of movement came from the closet, like the scratching of a small animal. Filled with dread, she slid the door open and there in one corner, crouched into a ball, she saw Heather, head down, her arms locked around her knees, still wearing a pink nightie stiff and crusty with splotches of dried blood.

"Pobrecita! O pobrecita mia!" She scooped the girl into her arms, the tightness of her hug matched by Heather's own, and the two clung to each other for wordless minutes while a terrible darkness began to form in Rosa's mind.

She could not think, did not want to think, or rather only wanted to think what she had thought at first, that the little girl had simply started her periods and was terrified of something she did not understand. But that was not right and she knew it. For one thing she was barely ten, small for her age, flat chested. Rosa herself had begun menstruating at eleven and that was considered early, even in Spain. But she had been chubby, with pert little breasts, with pubic hair; her time was early but not unique. No, this was something else, something she could not bear to think of as she rocked back and forth with the child, crooning, "Pobrecita!" over and over.

Then instinct took over. Rosa was a practical woman; she did not need to think, and in any case it was better not to think just now but to act. The child must be bathed and dressed. She started to put her down but the girl tightened her grip so painfully around the woman's neck that it would have been almost impossible to release her. Instinctively, Rosa understood.

"All right, it's all right," she murmured, carrying the child to and fro as she ran the bath, as she took folded clean underclothes from the drawer, as she took the school blouse and skirt from the closet and then discarded them for T-shirt and trousers. She moved back and forth across the hallway with as much stealth as she could, glancing with instinctive fear at the closed door of the master bedroom.

The child flinched with pain as she was lowered into the warm water but made no sound. Even then she continued to cling to Rosa's neck, making it difficult for the poor woman to use the flannel she was holding in one hand. But somehow she managed, watching the water turn a pale pink as she gently rubbed first one small leg and then the other. There didn't seem to be any fresh bleeding and she could feel the taut little body relaxing slightly with the warmth of the water and her own Spanish murmurs of comfort.

By the time she had wrapped the girl in a thick velvet

towel, still holding her close, she had formed a plan of her own. School would be impossible that day; so too would be remaining at home. She carried Heather into her room, helped her dress in the pale blue T-shirt and jeans, brushed the golden hair and tied it into a pony-tail. She had to accomplish the latter by sitting on the stool of the small white dressing table and looking into the mirror; the child still wanted to be held.

"Now I take you to Senora Fisher," Rosa said softly, matter-of-factly.

The girl nodded.

Rosa knew the Fisher house was nearby, for the two girls were often running back and forth to each other during half-terms and holidays, as were their brothers, Sebastian and Jeremy. In fact, she knew the street was the one beside the river, although she did not know the actual number of the house.

"You will show me the way," she said.

Again Heather nodded.

Rosa stood up with the girl in her arms and started across the landing for the stairway. As they passed the door of the master bedroom the child tightened her clasp around Rosa's already bruised neck and hid her face.

Sick at heart, Rosa needed no other proof.

* * * * *

It took fifteen minutes to reach the Fishers' house. Rosa was grateful that the rain had stopped, although it was still overcast and cold. She had carried Heather halfway before staggering to a stop.

"Nina, I think you must walk now," she panted.

Obediently the girl slid down Rosa's form to stand beside her. Reaching to take her hand, Rosa saw she was still clutching the square of cheese she had given her in place of breakfast, for she had shaken her head vehemently at the suggestion of cereal before they left. Rosa had understood that, for both of them were anxious to leave the house as soon as they could. But feeling the child should have something to eat, she had hurriedly cut off a piece of cheddar cheese and handed it to her to eat on the way. Now Rosa was worried to see she had not eaten it, had merely squeezed it into a sponge-like mass in her hand.

The pause was a long one after they rang the Fisher doorbell, long enough for Rosa to wish they had telephoned before setting out. She did not know what she would do if the Fisher Senora was not going to be in her house. That had never occurred to her.

Frantically she pressed the doorbell again. And again. Then Heather pressed it. It was not out of order; they could hear the long metallic buzz sounding through the house. And at last they could hear the miraculous sound of a chain being drawn back as the door finally swung open.

"Good heavens! Rosa! And Heather!" Susan Fisher stood before them in a yellow dressing gown, minus her make-up and looking older than Rosa would ever have thought. She was also leaning heavily on a cane, her right ankle thickly bandaged. "This," she gestured towards her foot as she prepared to make one of her witty remarks, "is -" But the remark dried on her lips. "What's wrong?" she asked. "Why are you here?"

"Please, Senora Fisher, is this all right if she can stay

here with you?"

Susan shifted her weight painfully on the cane, but she was, after all, a professional actress. "Of course," she answered, as if it were the most natural thing in the world to find her best friend's "daily" on her own doorstep at eight o'clock in the morning, along with her best friend's child who should have been on the way to school, both of them looking pale and distraught. "Come in."

She started to lead the way, hobbling with a slowness worthy of a snail, then stopped. "You'd better go ahead of me."

"Please, Senora, I will go back now, all right?"

"But Rosa -" She really wanted to know something more of the situation. "When do you - I mean, Judy isn't staying here right now because of this damned ankle, so she won't be back after school today and -" She stopped at the stricken look on Rosa's face.

"Of course I'm delighted Heather is here," she continued, "because she'll be the most wonderful help to me just now." She was indeed a consummate actress, she congratulated herself, noting Rosa's relief. "How long can she stay?" She needed to know. Obviously this was some kind of emergency, and she needed to know about that, too. Or at least, she wanted to. When was it Marinda was due back from that damned Retreat?

Rosa shrugged. "Octavian perhaps comes later for her. I do not know. Or Senora Marinda comes today or tomorrow perhaps."

"I see," said Susan with studied casualness and a bright smile in Heather's direction, although the child had been looking at the floor the entire time. Perhaps Michael had gone on a real bender with Marinda away, though it seemed odd to keep Heather away from school for that reason. "Then I'll just wait until I hear from you, okay?"

"Okay," Rosa nodded in relief.

"Are you sure you don't want some coffee or anything?"

"No, Senora, gracias." She bent down then to hug the little girl, who hugged her back with intense ferocity. She did not like to leave her, but at least she knew that here the child was safe. Gently she prized the small hand out of her own.

"Be good, pobrecita," she whispered.

The child nodded, still clutching the squadge of cheese in the tight fist of her other hand. For the first time it occurred to Rosa that the little girl had not spoken a single word since she had found her in the closet that morning.

"Can you see yourself out, Rosa? It'll take me forever to reach the door again."

Rosa nodded. She was grateful to the kind Senora and felt she should have told her more, though she did not know how to say it. Turning at the door, however, she made a belated attempt on her way out.

"Gracias, Senora, gracias. She must not be with her father."

Something in her tone made Susan's eyes widen in horror, a reaction she quickly stifled in the best thespian tradition. Then her eyes narrowed in the first faint realization of the possibility that just perhaps there could be in the world a man even worse than K.R.

XVIII

"Tell me, Rosa."

She was not surprised that the front door seemed to open electronically at her approach. She had seen the dining room curtain twitch as she got out of the car before Octavian sped away, and she knew then that her little Spanish 'daily' was lying in wait, watching for her.

With tears. For as soon as she stepped across the threshold Rosa threw both arms about her, emotion at last exploding into sobs as she wept with all the abandon and relief of the rescued.

"Senora, oh Senora!"

"Rosa, just a minute - wait, Rosa." She was trying to kick the door shut with her foot and she needed to set her holdall down. Another child seeking reassurance, she thought mindlessly as she drew back, and one whose hands were inexplicably black. Then in guilt she allowed herself to be hugged and briefly, woodenly, hugged back. It was obvious Michael had not yet returned.

"Tell me, Rosa."

Never had she seen such a change in anyone's face as in Rosa's in the three days they had been apart. The woman was cringing like an ill-treated dog, unable to look at her, tears welling up constantly in her eyes, spilling over and running down her cheeks as she tried to speak. But the words would not come.

Finally she plucked Marinda's sleeve and managed, "Come, I show you, Senora."

She led Marinda to her daughter's room, drew back the eiderdown and showed her the bloodstained sheets, for she had left them exactly as they were. Already the dried blood was taking on a brownish tinge.

For a second Marinda thought she was going to be sick and clutched the back of the chair, but this passed into a coldness so intense it was as if her body was packed in ice. But at least she was in control of it.

"There is more, Senora."

"More blood?" Dear God. "Where?"

"Not blood, no. But many times I see - there was ..." She stopped and the tears welled up again for she did not know how to say it, how to describe the stiff colourless stains she had noticed on the girl's sheets from time to time in the past. She cringed again, unable to meet the Senora's eyes.

"Culpa mia, Senora. I should have known. It is my fault because I should have known the other stains."

But she had not known. She had seen them, yes, and she had sensed uneasily that something was not as it should be, had even intended one day to ask the Senora about them. But it had seemed better to wait, to pretend they were not there; she had even thought perhaps they might go away if she said nothing, she had willed them to go away. And sometimes they had, sometimes for a week or more they would not be there at all. Only today, at last, had she made the connection between them and the stains on Juan's and Pilar's sheets which she took to the laundromat.

She wiped her eyes and her nose with her hand, leaving black streaks on her face. "My fault," she repeated.

Marinda took her shoulders. "Look at me, Rosa." She was surprised at the firmness of her own voice, at its sick calmness. "It was not your fault. You did not do this. You did not even know about this until today." One glance at the broken creature before her was proof of that. "And then you did the right thing. You took Heather away, out of the house, out of danger; you took her to Susan. That was a good thing, do you hear? It was the right thing to do. And you told Octavian. That was right, too, because he came to get me. These were all good things."

But, if anything, Rosa wept even harder at her exoneration, smearing her face further with her blackened hands until she resembled a kind of circus clown.

"Oh for God's sake, stop it, Rosa! Hush!" She spoke harshly as she took one of the rough black hands in her own, turning it over. The palm was even dirtier. It did not matter in the least but she asked the question anyway. "Why are your hands like this?"

"I clean the silver."

"I see. Fine. But now, Rosa, I want you to go home."

"Now?"

"Now."

"But the silver, she is everywhere all over in the kitchen. And the sheets. I must -"

"Leave the sheets. Leave the silver. I want to speak to -" she swallowed, unable to say 'my husband', nor yet to use his name. She settled for "- the Senor -" and continued, "when he comes in. I want to speak to him alone, you understand?"

Rosa nodded, hic-coughing now after so much sobbing. The Senora sounded strong and sure in a way she had never sounded before, but she looked very strange. Her face was white and each cheek had a bright red spot on it like a circle of paint. The spots had not been there when she first came home.

"I will go," Rosa said in a subdued voice, unbuttoning her smock, hic-coughing again.

"One thing more I must know. What did you say to - the Senor?"

"I do not speak with the Senor today."

Marinda nodded. "Wash your hands and face before you go. Hurry!" The abrupt orders were not typical. She looked at her watch but did not see it.

Minutes later she was alone in the house.

She used the bathroom. She walked up and down the hall. Twice. She climbed the stairs.

She walked to the door of Heather's room and stood there silently looking in.

She had painted a mural there once, a trellis of pink roses along one wall, a climbing rose across the ceiling. A bower of rosebuds for their rosebud Sleeping Beauty, a pink and white fairytale sanctuary.

No, not sanctuary. Prison. She had decorated a prison. A torture chamber.

The child had tried to tell her - what was it she had said? Nightmares. I can't tell you about my nightmares, she had said. Not when Daddy's there. Because Daddy was the nightmare. She remembered her daughter's white, pinched face, so anxious that afternoon at their pretend picnic in the drawing room. Anxious and frightened. Trying to tell her. Trying to say help me.

She turned as her stomach heaved, ran to the basin across the hall, vomited. Afterwards splashed cold water on her face. Shakily walked back down the stairs. Cold, so very cold.

Into the kitchen. Yes, as Rosa had said, silver everywhere. She touched a tray with the toe of her shoe, moved it slightly to one side. It did not matter. None of it mattered.

Back into the study. He had been there. Oh yes. There was the unwashed glass, the thin film of Scotch in its base. There was this morning's newspaper, open on the edge of the desk.

She would wait. She would be certain first. Beyond any - what was the legal phrase? - shadow of doubt.

* * * * *

And forgiveness? Was that waiting, too? How odd her quest had been. Pointless. Premature, the wrong way round. She had sought the answer before the question had been asked. Driven why? Premonition?

With sudden violence the face of Brother David formed before her, a volcano pushing upward through the crust of consciousness. 'I will tell you what forgiveness is,' his mouth was saying. But with a violence as sudden as his appearance she wrenched his face out of her memory, gritting her teeth.

She would not listen, would not see, would not remember, would not think. Because she knew. She knew that definitions of forgiveness were pointless. She had encountered the thing not possible to forgive.

And she waited.

* * * * *

He came not much later, key in the lock, steps in the hall, scent of alcohol like a sour, faintly sick perfume surrounding him, preceding him as he leaned into the study where she was sitting.

He gave an involuntary start as he saw her, narrowing his eyes.

"What are you doing here?"

"I live here. Remember?" What stage had he reached in his drinking? She needed him to be aware, fully cognizant. She prayed for that, just that.

"Live here? Not in my study, you don't." The thin upper lip rose in a faint sneer.

Good. However slowed by Garrick wine, still capable of sarcastic repartee, still perfectly capable of understanding. That was important. "The study is where you come first," she said icily, "which is why I'm here."

"Indeed?" The sneer was now fully formed. "It's easy to see your little trip to Lourdes hasn't cured you. You're still a bitch."

She ignored the taunt. "I want to talk to you."

He moved towards the liquor cabinet but she stood up and moved in front of it, facing him. The uncharacteristic behaviour surprised him; he stopped beside the desk. Once she would have been afraid of him, primitively afraid of his height and size. No longer. She herself was the giant now, an Amazon of ice, fully in control, the one calling the shots. She was not afraid. Because when the worst thing has already happened there is absolutely nothing left to be afraid of.

"I want to talk to you," she repeated.

"Then talk." He leaned against the desk, folding his arms across his chest in the deafening body language of defence.

"About Heather." Would he deny it? Plead lack of memory? Was there still some possible - please God, let there be - alternate explanation even now, even beyond belief?

His eyes narrowed. "So?"

He was going to make her say it. She reached one hand out blindly for support, found the bronze bust on the plinth, the head of the other Michael, and steadied herself.

"You raped her."

He did not answer. Mouth slightly open, he stood focused on nothing, glazed eyes glued to the wall behind her left shoulder, while unbelievable minutes ticked by. One. Two. Three. How incredibly slow they were. She had not expected this, had expected anything but this. Four. Five. She would not be the one to speak first, would not beg for an answer, although her own invincible ice armour was beginning a hairline crack and the loudest scream in the universe was not far away. Seven minutes. Why didn't he speak? Her eyes never left his face, the sagging open mouth, the puffy, unseeing eyes. Was he wondering how she knew? Inventing an alibi? Overcome with shame and remorse?

"Moral absolutes," he said finally with cold venom, and the eyes that turned on her at last were the cold grey eyes of a snake.

Rimmed by pink. (Even then, unwitting and unwanting, one part of her mind was mixing the colour on a palette, inventing a new shade, Alcoholic Carmine.)

"You have always been guilty of moral absolutes."

She had never heard so much hatred in a voice before. And it continued:

"If you weren't such a puritanical Baptist, locked into your silly little code of conduct -"

Baptist? Why Baptist? Her mind seized on the irrelevance, protective, unwilling to let herself hear whatever else he might be saying. She had never been inside a Baptist church; come to think of it, had never even seen one, did not know what Baptists believed.

"- then you'd know there are other views of sexual morality, a whole spectrum of possibilities. The Egyptian kings, the Greek gods ..."

The man was mad. No, he was onstage, playing Ramses II, playing Zeus.

"I did not rape my daughter." He spat out the word rape. "She's been asking for it for years."

No! No! Untrue! But her protest emerged only as a choking kind of strangulated half cough, ignored and unheard.

"She's always flirted with me. She's known what she was doing, subconscious or not."

He was speaking more rapidly now, as if in a hurry to

get it said, his face growing a dull red with excitement. This was a man she did not know.

"And if you'd like to know," he went on huskily, thickly, "it's been like tasting a new wine, smooth and perfect - and one I've made myself." The thin lips twisted into a leer at his double entendre as if expecting appreciation from her, as if expecting approval.

She had never noticed how yellow his teeth had become. But he was not mad. Not acting. This was the face of evil. Pure evil.

"It's hardly what I've been used to. Tears don't turn me on." He was deliberately taunting her now. "You could never wait for me to pull out, could you? Did you think I didn't notice that or your bloody tears? What good have you been, except for priming?"

Then a new thought seemed to cross his mind and he narrowed his eyes. "How did you find out? Did she tell you?"

Beyond the accusation was the whisper of a threat in the child's direction. Threat, intimidation. Don't tell. How had he dared? She shook her head in an almost imperceptible reflex, staring at him fascinated, mouse to cobra. But only for an instant before her strength returned tenfold.

"Then how did you find out?"

"The blood." Let him deal with that.

He seemed surprised. "Ah well," he shrugged, smug, self-satisfied, "it was dark. I suppose since it was the first full ..." his voice trailed off, "...last night may have surprised her, may have hurt a little."

Then inclining his head in justification, he continued. "She probably thought it was a dream. She'll learn to like it. I've gone slowly with her. One day she'll thank me for breaking her in."

And those were the last words he ever uttered.

For the ice woman in the study picked up the bronze bust of the man before her and smashed it into his head. For a split-second his face registered astonishment and disbelief, then a mini-second of fear, before the eyes rolled back in his head and he fell heavily to the floor.

She stood above him, still holding the bust. It was as heavy as a cannon ball, but to her, the ice goddess, it had no weight at all as she lifted it high in the air again, high above her own head, and brought it crashing down once more onto the left side of his skull.

It was like striking a hard unripe melon. There was a dull thwacking sound and yes, it split above the ear, making an indentation like the hollow of a half grapefruit. For a second she could see through the crack into his skull and it looked like the inside of a pomegranate, clotted red jewels set in white pith, but then the blood came surging forth in a great wave and she could no longer see anything else.

He had knocked the newspaper off the desk as he fell and was now lying partially across it. She watched the blood flow across the newsprint, blotting out letters as it spread, swallowing headlines, then stories. Now it was obliterating the weather forecast at the bottom of the page and she had to read exceptionally fast to keep ahead of it ... Gale force winds ... Heavy rain ... Brighter later ...

XIX

Afterwards she sat for a long time at the desk, exhausted but curiously at peace. Her mind, which for so long had darted about unable to concentrate on anything, had finally alighted and was still.

There were decisions to be made now, of course. The room would have to be dealt with, the body, the sodden newspaper, eventually the reddened, ruined carpet. Practicalities. Someone should be contacted, but who first? Police? Funeral Directors? God? No. He already knew.

Somewhere deep inside her something stirred, as light and faint as a butterfly's wing, reminiscent of the first quickening of her first child. It was the first tentative, inexplicable breath of grief. But nothing like the wild beating of wings and claws that came afterward, much later, after everyone had finally left, the voices, the stretcher, the siren and footsteps and lights and words, when she had finally gone and stood alone in the closet among Michael's clothes, his shirts, the smell of him, beyond the alcohol. And wept.

That was long after the doorbell had rung the first time, when she was still sitting in the study, drained, looking at the crumpled body in its pool of blood. It was after she had gone to answer the door, opening it to the balding Reverend Sam and Emma in her horn-rimmed glasses. It was after wondering why they should be standing there at all, looking so concerned.

But she had numbly told them, "I've just killed my husband."

XX

"But, of course, he didn't die."

The two old friends were sitting in one of the monastery's inner rooms with two mugs of tea on the small table in front of them.

"By the grace of God." Brother David was in his favourite position, straddling a chair backwards, his arms folded along its top. "I wouldn't have liked to see her in prison."

"No," the Reverend Sam agreed. "That's mainly thanks to you."

"You mean because I phoned you?"

"Absolutely. It meant we were first on the scene, and nobody ever questioned our version of events. It would have been a different matter if he'd died. But, of course, he didn't die."

It was winter of 1994, two years after the Daily Mail had run a page two article under the headline, "Actor's Freak Accident", describing how Michael Lawson had tripped in his home and fallen heavily against a bronze bust of himself, which had in turn toppled over on him again as he lay on the floor.

Although the paper did not mention a drinking problem, that was taken for granted by his friends and acquaintances, and in fact, the entire entertainment world, as being the true cause of the accident. No one who knew him would have guessed otherwise, particularly since the parish priest and his wife had apparently been visiting the Lawsons at the time; they were the ones who had called the ambulance.

There had been a follow-up article the next day, reporting the actor in a coma in intensive care at Charing Cross Hospital. After that there was nothing for three months, and then only a small inside paragraph announcing that the actor Michael Lawson had been transferred to the Atkinson Morley Hospital in Wimbledon for treatment following a head injury in October.

In fact he had remained in a coma for all of those three months, and it was only when he had finally emerged into a dim world of consciousness, damaged but no longer endangered, that he had been sent to Britain's top neurological hospital for assessment as to the extent of brain damage, and for possible, if partial, rehabilitation.

For the first six months after it happened the Reverend Sam had called at the monastery regularly, keeping his friend in touch. But gradually the visits had tapered off; there were occasional phone calls but they had not seen each other now since August.

And this was a farewell visit, for Sam was shortly leaving both the priesthood and the Church of England, and was moving to Bristol with his family.

Both had seen it coming in the violent upheaval the Church of England had suffered since the Ordination of Women Measure had become canon law in 1992. There had been a massive steady exodus of both clergy and laity.

"I thought at first I could stick it out," Reverend Sam told him. "Such a lot at stake, you know, including the house. And my so-called vocation." He laughed bitterly.

"But in the end I couldn't."

"Ah. The cost of conscience."

"Right. You know that's an organization?"

"I know."

"I got so tired of trying to explain - mostly to non-believers and non-church goers - that it isn't a case of simple misogyny on my part. They were always telling me women can preach as well as men. Of course they can. Often better."

"What was the sticking point for you?"

"Thinking of a woman holding up the bread, saying, 'This is my body given for you', knowing she wouldn't be representing the congregation at that point, but representing J.C. And J.C. wasn't a woman, as simple as that."

Brother David nodded but did not speak.

"And then having them say, 'Oh, but if J.C. had been born today it would have been different,' and realizing they don't really believe J.C. was God at all, stepping into his own creation, capable of choosing the time He wanted. There's no argument possible for non-believers; if you don't really believe in the Incarnation of course it doesn't make sense. I'm just so tired of it, that's all."

But it wasn't really all. He was tired, too, of the weak and vacillating stance of the C. of E. on almost every major moral issue. He remembered another conversation, again about the ordination of women, when the woman had said - actually it was Susan Fisher, whose visit to the Lawson house had coincided recently with one of his own, and who had said, "I really don't understand it. It's just like abortion; people used to be up in arms about that, too, but now it's accepted as a right for all women if they want one. It's the same with the ordination of women. In another twenty years everyone will wonder what all the fuss was about!"

And he had felt an enormous tiredness spreading through his body, he had been too tired even to make a reply to the woman, with her stage make-up and booming theatrical voice, and anyway, he had reflected, her prophecy was probably true. In twenty years who would care? He supposed he would, but it was a losing battle.

For himself he did not want to be part of an organization which condoned as a right the ripping apart of an unborn child, any more than he wanted to be among those who championed the right of a woman to be priested. But it was happening. Socially present, politically correct. He thought of the days of his own ordination, long gone, when vocation had been considered divine, no one's right. When abortion had been considered a sin. No one's right. (He had written his bishop once for the 'official' stance of the C. of E. on that particular issue in order to quote it in a sermon; the reply - from the bishop's chaplain - had stated there was no official stance, that it was a matter for individual conscience.) No, it was time for him to go, to pull the tattered remnants of his faith about him and leave, before that went, too.

His friend had remained silent.

"What about you?" the Reverend Sam asked. "Hasn't this hit your Order?"

"The Ordination of Women?"

"Yes."

"Of course. Not that they'll be applying as novices here," he smiled, "but as for the validity of their Orders, whether we would - or could - receive communion at the hand of a woman ... We're split right down the middle. I don't know what's going to happen. To me the real tragedy is the schism itself."

For a time they sat in agreeable silence and then the monk spoke again.

"Do you know what you'll be doing?"

"No idea. Emma has a job lined up with the Social Services in Bristol."

"Then she agrees with you?"

"Not entirely. But she loves me."

"Perhaps you'll go to Rome."

"Not unless I can be sure of going towards it, not just away from the C. of E. Running to, not from."

"Conscience again."

"I suppose so."

"That's why we're friends."

Sam nodded.

"What about Marinda Lawson? Will you keep in touch with her?"

"We'll try, but geography is bound to make a difference."

"I wish she would come back to see me."

"She's never contacted you since?" And when Brother David shook his head the priest commented, "I'm surprised. But then it was such an abrupt end to everything for her, not just the Retreat."

"Quite. The son came to get her, you know - Octavian - but he didn't go into detail, just told Brother Thaddeus it was a crisis. I would never have known the full story if it hadn't been for you. I wrote to her after you told me what happened, but she didn't reply."

"I'm so glad you phoned as she left."

"She was obviously going to need help. I didn't know how much."

Reverend Sam stuffed tobacco into his pipe. A few shreds fell on the floor. "Em and I were surprised that - well, having tried to kill him, she's now taking care of him."

"I'm not entirely surprised. She took her marriage vows seriously. And she learned about atonement here."

"Of course she's had some time to adjust to it all, that three months while he was in a coma, and then another six while he was being rehabilitated at the Atkinson Morley. But she never went near him in all that time. Not a single visit until the day I took her to collect him."

"How is she coping now, after two years?"

"Pretty well, I'd say. He's like a child, you know, a two-year-old. Requires constant attention. She has help, of course, that Spanish daily, and there's a retired nurse who comes in the afternoons."

"What about nights?"

"She's on her own."

"Can he speak?"

"A few words but they don't make much sense. Baby talk."

"What about the children?"

Sam drew deeply on his pipe. "There was never going to be a problem with the three who were away. They came back - Septimus from his Stateside tour, Julian and Sebastian from their schools - and were told about their father's tragic accident. They accepted it all without question - as children do - and they rallied, as children do. And now Septimus is at Cambridge and Julian and Sebastian are back in their schools."

"Good."

"That was the only way we could convince Marinda to lie about what happened. By telling her the kids would lose both parents, not just one. That all the kids would be traumatized, not just one. She wanted to ring the police right away and confess everything. Of course at that point she thought he was dead. We all did."

Brother David made no comment.

"It was Emma who talked her out of phoning," he said proudly. "I went in the ambulance with Michael."

"I remember your telling me that. What about the other two?"

"Octavian might suspect the truth but he'll never know for sure whether it was an accident or not. It's a lot harder for him to accept the other. He knows that's true. But I understand he never sees his father, won't go into that room when he visits. I doubt if he's told anyone why, even his brothers. But you must know all this; he comes here, doesn't he?"

"He comes to see Brother Thaddeus, not me."

"Ah."

"And he sometimes comes to Mass."

"That's great."

The other shrugged. "Heavenly serendipity. I had thought his mother would be the one to come," and here he smiled disarmingly, "but one should never attempt to guess the mind of God."

"She does go to Mass every day."

"Where?" The monk seemed surprised.

"St Mary's, Bourne Street."

"Good place, but a long way off."

"Well, as you know, our only Communion service is on the third Sunday of the month." And now it was the Reverend Sam's turn to chuckle. "I've always known she preferred a high church, and I've heard St. Mary's is as high as you'll ever get without drugs."

Brother David laughed. "Not a bad description. But it's a good place. They come to us for an annual Retreat. And I suppose I'm not really surprised to hear she's going there."

"Why do you say that?"

"Because I always saw her as a natural Catholic, well on her way to Rome. She's pretty close at St. Mary's - may not go any further. Doctrinally, she could, of course, but that's not the way her mind functions. It's quite a trek for her though, from Barnes. Must be a sixteen mile round trip. You say she goes every day?"

"She drives in early every morning just after seven, before the rush-hour traffic, and she's back by eight-thirty."

"Then she can leave him alone?"

"Not really. The Spanish daily comes early now, at seven o'clock."

The monk raised black eyebrows. "That's loyalty for you."

"She was devoted to the family." Reverend Sam pictured the squat little figure who had so obviously transferred allegiance to Marinda, serving and guarding her as fiercely and protectively as a spaniel. The odds were that her own Catholic priest knew a thing or two about the situation, but he would never know.

"What about the little girl?"

"More difficult, as you might guess. She stayed with the Fishers at first, her best friend's family. I think I told you that. Marinda was frantic to have her back, living under her own roof again, but it took time, lots of little visits back and forth before it finally happened."

"Was that the Social Services' idea?"

"The social services were never told about any of it, certainly not the abuse. There was no point with the danger past - and anyway Emma was doing a lot of unobtrusive counselling."

The monk merely nodded.

"It was a funny thing, though - apparently the child thought her father was dead. We didn't realize that for a long time."

Again the monk nodded. "Of course. He wasn't there. Probably nobody mentioned him but she would have sensed something terrible had happened. So how did she find out he was still alive?"

"She saw the hospital bed being delivered the day before he came home and asked what it was for. Marinda told her but she didn't say anything else, at least not then, just hid behind her mother and watched as they carried him in on a stretcher. She stared for a long time and then finally whispered, 'Is that Daddy?' and Marinda said it was."

The man was silent for a time before continuing, almost as an afterthought. "But then the most extraordinary thing. Marinda didn't see her do it but thinks it must have been her. A jam jar with flowers, on the floor just inside the door of his room. Flowers from the garden, the stems too short, the way a child picks them. That was all and just the once."

"It was enough," said the monk.

"I gather she always avoided the room after that, so maybe the flowers weren't her after all. Anyway, she's in boarding school now - as of September. Some place near Ascot - Heathfield, I think."

"Was that always planned?"

"I think so, but they managed to bring it forward a year. Judy Fisher was going up at the same time and it's good the girls are together. Who knows how it will all turn out eventually? Everything changes. I mean, who would have guessed two years ago that Octavian would be so successful onstage? Anything can happen."

"So it can."

The other rose to go. "I don't suppose you will ever visit Bristol."

"Anything can happen," the taller man smiled, and for the first time the Reverend Sam noticed how much grey was in his hair. "I wish you luck. I will keep you in my prayers."

"And I you." That at least was true, Reverend Sam reflected. He had not lost sight of the Almighty, merely the Almighty's church.

As the two men walked together down the wide hallway with the red geraniums glowing at the end, Brother David spoke again.

"She was trying to work through it, you know, the whole issue of forgiveness. I wonder if she ever made it."

The other hesitated. "Hard to say. She doesn't talk to me on that level. I can only go by what I see, and from what I see, she's coping fairly well. She's taken up her painting again, quite seriously. Even has an exhibition coming up."

By this time they had reached the door of the conservatory where they parted with a handshake. As the Reverend Sam crunched across the gravel beside the little statue of the laughing St Francis, the monk called after him.

"Tell her to get in touch with me."

Perhaps he was puzzled, perhaps even hurt in a small way, the Reverend Sam reflected, that she had not done so.

XXI

Marinda sat quietly in the room which had been the study. It was just after five o'clock, already deep dusk, although the darkness was beginning to come noticeably a little later each day. She was always glad when the winter solstice had passed.

She rose to turn on the gas-fired logs in the fireplace, more for the welcoming light they would give than their slight warmth. The fire sprang to life at her touch, eternal flames flowing over eternal logs in parody of a Victorian hearth. Then she returned to her chair and the circle of lamplight cast by the lamp with the yellow shade.

The study itself had been transformed. The fireplace was still there and the shelves of books, but the desk had been pushed to one wall, next to the chair where she now sat, and wide cork tiles had replaced the carpet on the floor. A large hospital bed with a white metal frame dominated the centre of the room. A wheelchair was folded neatly in the corner by the door.

The liquor cabinet had been replaced by a wash-basin and the space around it enlarged to include a closet. The mirrored wall was still visible behind a man's robe and two empty hangers, but the music that had once tinkled forth at the touch of a latch was gone forever.

Michael himself was asleep in the bed, the shadow of his profile magnified huge and sharp on the wall. The nurse had gone home, as always, at five o'clock. Rosa, who still came to clean in the mornings and to help out generally, had left at twelve.

Marinda would sit in the room now for perhaps an hour; later she would bring the tray with the food which Rosa had carefully cut up and prepared before she left. Then she would help Michael to eat, for he had trouble guiding the spoon to his mouth. If she didn't give him a spoon he could eat with his hands fairly well, but this wasn't always practical, depending on the menu.

It had been a good day. Usually she painted in the mornings but today she had gone to see Brother David instead. She had thought of doing this from time to time over the past two years but somehow the time was never right and the original urgency which had driven her was no longer there.

There were other reasons, too, only half defined, the fear of the recognition of an icon and its disproportionate influence on the new-found freedom of her thinking. But these were merely half-thoughts, unformulated and uncertain, translating themselves only into a vague kind of procrastination. But Sam, a frequent caller here now in his penultimate days, had been to the monastery last week and had told her she must go herself, that it was not right to leave so many things unsaid and undone.

So she had gone this morning, driving through the wintry park quietly and calmly, without a single sighting of Henry VIII or his deer. The park had been bleak and grey, the trees black lace against the sky.

"And forgiveness?" the monk had asked. "Have you been able to forgive him?"

"He has no memory, Brother David. So how is it possible?"

"No memory whatsoever?"

"Not from before. He remembers nothing, not himself or me or the house or anything at all. He recognizes me now only as someone who is there, who helps to feed him, that's all. He is beyond understanding the simplest thing. He has no idea, no concept of what he has done. So how can you either punish or forgive someone who doesn't know what he has done?"

"You have already punished. It now remains to forgive."

"But how can I forgive him when he doesn't know what he's done?"

"Father, forgive them for they know not what they do?"

"That was different. The Roman soldiers were at least capable of knowing what they did, and certainly they did know on one level. Okay, they may not have understood they were driving nails through the incarnate flesh of God himself, but they certainly knew they were driving nails through human flesh and that it was causing pain. Michael isn't capable of grasping - even if he were told - the concept of rape or even of sex, let alone incest. I don't know if he's even the same person - whether it's Michael lying there - this thing without a memory."

"Of course it is. Identity is more than memory."

"Then I don't know how it is possible to forgive him."

"It doesn't have to be two ways. You can offer forgiveness whether he can receive it or not."

"Define forgiveness."

"I did that for you once."

"Yes, you told me that forgiving was seeing the person

- the unforgiven - as God intended him to be. In that sense, perhaps it is possible. Because he is so simple now, like a small child. Everything pleases him. He laughs at sunbeams. He is now, I suppose, within these limitations, a good person. If recognizing that constitutes forgiving, then perhaps, perhaps I do. And yet - there is always what he has done."

"And what you have done."

"I went to Confession."

"St Mary's, Bourne Street?"

"Yes."

"And you were absolved."

"Yes."

"So God has forgiven you. Have you forgiven yourself?"

The question had surprised her and she recognized it for the trick it was, the same ultimate trap of pride which had snapped shut on Judas Iscariot.

"I don't know," she answered slowly. "I did what should have been done. I don't know what else I could have done. I meant it to be an execution. If I could have done it differently, ideally, well, I mean if only I were God - (She smiled now, remembering the flinch of surprised amusement on Brother David's face as she spoke those words) - I would simply have sentenced him to a lifetime - no, an eternity - of knowing what he'd done. Punishment enough. But Michael was never going to realize that, not with all his drinking, not ever. And what he did was monstrous beyond belief." Her voice hardened. "I did what needed to be done."

229

"And you have forgiven him," the monk said softly, "because you are tending him now."

"Expiation of guilt, perhaps."

"Expression of love, perhaps. And no, I'm not going to define love, because it has no definition."

* * * * *

Yes, it had been a good visit, she reflected now in the study, a wholesome, healing, satisfactory meeting of minds.

She would not return. He had asked her to come back but she had looked at him, straight at the centre of his eyes and given her answer.

"No. I'm not going to risk the second commandment."

For a fleeting second there was amused comprehension in his eyes and far beneath that the merest sliding shadow of something else, unnamed and undefined, moved quickly and was gone.

She had her own wisdom. Like most women the core of its foundation was intuition, that infallible sense elusive to the mark and measure of science; instinctively she knew the time to end anything was before it began. Her thoughts, collected now and clear, had coalesced into definition. And she had the satisfaction of knowing that each of them thought the other remarkable as they said goodbye. He did not even shake her hand. But he made the sign of the cross as he blessed her.

* * * * *

It was all as it should be, she thought now in the firelit study. She would continue to grow in her thinking, to follow the path this finest of teachers had indicated and it would lead to myriad other paths, branching and winding but leading always onward, upward, Godward. She would paint along the way and she would grieve for her lost and injured child and her life would not be easy.

Just because she had encountered the worst of problems did not mean there would not be others. She knew now without it ever having been said that Octavian had confronted his homosexuality, had discovered through a chance meeting with Brother Thaddeus that he need not act upon it, had discovered the priceless truth that in order to love it was not necessary to possess, even momentarily. The immeasurable joy of his relief had poured into his acting, had been sublimated into the sublime; his talent was already becoming incandescent. But his life, too, would be not easy and the burden of his father a lifelong weight.

And who knew what would become of the others? There would be problems, serious, perhaps insurmountable. Sebastian already was drinking secretly, that she knew, too, following the pattern laid down by his father, superimposed intractably on his young life. What was it Al-Anon called alcoholism? Oh yes, The Family Disease.

She looked at her husband, who shifted and stirred beneath the sheet but did not waken. Only gradually had she come to realize that her own impossible prayer had been answered. Make Michael as he used to be. And the terrible knowledge with which he could not have lived had been taken away, had been replaced by the innocence of Eden, a simple delight in all things. She had not even dreamed of that, miracle indeed. It was not really what she had asked for, not what she had meant.

But he was as he used to be, perhaps even before he was born. Outwardly, too, his face was unlined, the puffiness gone away, the silhouette on the wall revealing the fine clear features of an earlier day.

Yes, he was recognizably the Michael who used to be. But it still was not quite that Michael, the first Michael, with his wit and charm and impossible ideals who was lying before her now. Nor was it the second, the cruelly articulate, bloated and alcoholic Michael who had done such a terrible thing. No, it was a third Michael before her now and somehow all three were caught together in the web of time and linked by memory, hers if not his. And to which of them had she promised "until death us do part"?

Time and memory were inter-dependent, perhaps they were even the same. And Michael had escaped them both, but she had not. She would go on through time and she would grieve forever for her lost and broken child and she would pray for her without ceasing. But not all prayers were answered, or at least not recognizably, that much she knew. "But you never know the end of the story," Brother David had once said. And that was true.

She looked at the figure of her sleeping husband, breathing deeply, regularly in the hospital bed. He was tired, for he had been in the wheelchair today, and sitting always tired him. He could take it for no more than an hour at a time and it took two of them, usually herself and the nurse, to manoeuvre him into it, and strap him carefully so he would not fall out.

How he loved being pushed, loved the change of the street with its cars and people! They would push him fast, so that the wind ruffled his hair and he would smile all the way.